Imposter

Helen Dale

ISBN 978-1-7397667-2-6

Acknowledgements

I am grateful to members of Manchester Women's Writers' group for their critiques of many of the chapters and to Linda and Sharon for their comments on the completed novel.

Cover illustration 1936583 © Starfotograf | Dreamstime.com

Authentic Stories of the Transgender Community Series

Authentic stories featuring transgender characters. The series are generally stand-alone books - though characters may well appear in more than one book (eg Jacqui is in both Summer Dreams and Operation Busted Flush). Most can be read in any order. The exceptions are the Impact Series which are planned as a trilogy.

The author identified as a cross dresser for decades before accepting that she needed to transition permanently in the mid-1990s. In that time, she has attended trans groups and met trans people from all over the UK (and abroad); she has run several trans and LGBT groups and has been a counsellor specialising in gender variant clients for more than twenty years. She has served on local and national diversity boards for the Probation and Prison services, Police and Crown Prosecution Service and has provided trans awareness training for a diverse range of organisations. Socially she has met hundreds, if not thousands, of trans individuals each with their own story.

This, together with her own experiences, has provided her with a wealth of details on which to base her novels and ensure that they are absolutely authentic.

Chapter 1.   Nathan

Nathan Poulson strode purposefully along the High Street. His bearing, close-cropped haircut, highly polished shoes, smartly ironed shirt, neatly pressed grey trousers and blazer, complete with regimental badge and tie, marking him out as a former soldier.

As he passed an Asian food store, he turned his face away from the repellent invasion of what used to be a traditional English area. Smelling the stink of curry and other spices emanating from the open doorway, he spat in the gutter, then held his breath as he walked by.

He was heading for the Nelson's Arms and a meeting with Peter Holmes the leader of 'Action 4 England', an organisation dedicated to the repatriation of all foreigners, especially non-white races. In his own mind, the jury was still out on whether that should include Celts and Irish. Some, of course, regarded him as racist. He considered himself to be a true patriot.

Entering the pub, he took the stairs two at a time up to the room A4E had borrowed for the afternoon. He was proud of his fitness and worked on it with six–mile runs most days – none of this 10-kilometre business for him.

He knocked on the door before opening it and walked briskly to the front of the desk behind which Holmes was sitting. Coming to attention he stood waiting for his commander to acknowledge him. He focused his eyes on the flag suspended on the wall behind his leader. It featured the red cross of St George on a white field. In the centre was a white circle outlined in red with A4E, the initials of Action 4 England, also in red within the circle. The left-hand upright of the 4 was vertical so that the upper left-hand quarter of the digit resembled a swastika.

"Nathan, thank you for coming so promptly. I have an important task for you."

"Sir!" Poulson responded, conditioned by his fifteen years in the army.

"Relax, Nathan. Pull up a chair."

Poulson picked up an upright chair from its place by the wall and placed it three feet away from the centre of Holmes' desk then sat down, straightening the creases of his trousers as he did so. He placed his hands palms down on each knee.

"Who do you think are the main enemies of true English Patriots, Nathan?"

"Immigrants, sir. Coming here and forcing their rules and culture, if you can call it that, on our people, sir."

"Wrong, Nathan. Oh, they *are* our enemies but they're not the main ones."

"Sir?" questioned Poulson.

"No, Nathan. The real enemies are the traitors within our own communities who don't acknowledge the threats posed to our way of life. Those who know the threat exists but are too wishy-washy to do anything about it. They're the real threat."

"Yes, sir. You're right, of course."

"The question is, how far are we prepared to go to deal with those traitors? How far are YOU personally prepared to go?"

Poulson leapt to his feet and stood rigidly to attention in front of Holmes.

"I'll do whatever is necessary, sir," he said firmly.

"You were in the army, weren't you?"

"Yes sir. Rank of corporal, sir."

"I believe you were in Iraq and Afghanistan? So, you'll have seen action?"

"Yes sir. Three tours."

He didn't mention that he'd been a clerk in Regimental Headquarters and the only time he'd shot a rifle had been on the range. He'd still been in theatre and had the medals to show for it.

"If I asked you to do something that resulted in the death of some of the traitors, how would you react?"

"You only have to give the order, sir."

"I thought that would be your answer. I've been watching you, Nathan. I've seen how committed you are to the cause. This is your opportunity to serve your country far more than you ever did in the army."

"Thank you, sir."

"You are going to attack delegates travelling to the Tory party conference in Manchester. You'll be dressed as an Arab so that it looks like a terrorist attack. That should anger many of the delegates at the conference and force their leaders to take a harder line on immigration. I gather you speak some Arabic?"

"Yes sir, enough to get by. Won't the presence of an Arab make the other passengers suspicious?"

"Very perceptive of you, Nathan. That's why you'll be disguised as a westernised Arab – as though you're a representative of one of the Arab states attending the conference to do business with defence industry exhibitors."

Poulson nodded his head.

"I see, sir."

"You'll join the 10.20 train at Euston. You'll have a reservation, in the name of Nasrallah Abedi, in one of the first-class coaches amongst the delegates. The name means 'Victory of God' – which will fit in with a terrorist attack."

"Very clever, sir."

"You'll join as soon as the train is ready and put your suitcase in the rack with the pockets facing outwards. Is that clear?"

"Crystal clear, sir."

"Five minutes after the train leaves Stoke on Trent station, you'll get out of your seat, leaving your raincoat and hat and go to the luggage rack where you'll appear to put something into the front pocket of your suitcase. In fact, you will activate the timer on the bomb. You'll then leave the coach and go through into the standard-class accommodation. As you've left your raincoat, it's unlikely anyone will think anything of it. If they do, they'll assume you are going to the toilet or the buffet car."

Holmes paused to light a cigarette.

"Leave the train at Macclesfield from one of the standard-class coaches. In case the staff at Macclesfield wonder why you're leaving the train before your destination; we'll provide both first-class tickets from Euston to Manchester and standard-class tickets from Stoke to Macclesfield. Don't mix them up."

"No, sir."

"The bomb will be timed to explode a few minutes after leaving Macclesfield. You'll be met outside the station and brought back to London. Any questions?"

"Where do I get the disguise and the suitcase, sir?"

Holmes picked up the phone and instructed his deputy, Tommy James, to join him.

"Tommy, I've briefed Nathan, take him round to the flat and get him sorted," Holmes ordered. "Then, meet me at the office."

When the two of them met an hour later, Tommy accepted the cigar that Holmes offered him.

"It's a pity we've got to lose Poulson, he's been a good reliable man," he remarked.

"True, but this is a vital job and, let's face it, he'd be quite a risk afterwards if he was questioned."

Tommy blew smoke rings at the ceiling.

"I know. And I realise we need to make sure the bomb goes off and timers aren't always reliable. There's no alternative but to have Poulson set it off when he thinks he's just activating the timer. With luck, it'll look like a premature detonation. Not going to be much of him left to sort through after the explosion."

Chapter 2.   Michelle

The Gulf Air Boeing Dreamliner took off on time and, as it climbed out of Bahrain, Michelle Hartley started to relax in her Falcon Gold Class seat. As soon as she could, she fully reclined the seat, lay out and tried to sleep. The business class upgrade hadn't been cheap – it was more than four times the price of an economy ticket; but the last few days had been nerve-wracking and she felt she deserved a bit of pampering.

She'd been managing an IT Project for an investment company in one of the new skyscrapers in Dubai's central business district. The Managing Director, Gerard Marshall, had been a misogynistic bastard and her project team had picked up on his attitude and had made her task as difficult as possible. Peter Gunn, the Senior User on her Project Board, had repeatedly promised to undertake tasks allocated to him – then consistently failed to do so. Deadlines had been missed, costs had escalated; for which the MD blamed her; and the whole experience had been more stressful than any other project she'd been involved in.

It had come to a head when Marshall instructed her to attend a party where one of the guests had assumed she was part of the entertainment. She'd rowed with Marshall and had been tempted to tell him, there and then, what he could do with the job – but the company was likely to insist on her working out the months' notice and Marshall wasn't likely to let his scapegoat escape so easily.

There'd been a risk that he'd have the authorities impose a travel ban which could prevent her from leaving the country if he'd realised she was planning to return to the UK. She'd pretended to be just attending an overnight meeting in Bahrain and had arranged for her belongings to be collected from her apartment once her flight had taken off.

She was glad to be heading back to the UK, for all its faults, to take up a new job in Salford Quays near Manchester. The Project Director, Sylvia Farrell, had interviewed her over Zoom. The connection hadn't been good and they'd had to switch off the video link and continue with audio only for much of the session. Fortunately, Sylvia had worked with Marshall and Gunn previously, knew what they were like and had focussed on Michelle's previous work.

The recruitment agency involved in the placement had recommended accommodation in a new high-rise development in the Quays and Michelle had been able to arrange a viewing and agree the lease online from Dubai. The apartment was only three hundred yards from the office with the Metro literally on the doorstep – as Michelle had discovered when she checked out the local area on the internet. She'd also found a good selection of bars and restaurants around the Quays.

It was only when the Dreamliner touched down on the runway at Heathrow, Michelle felt she could really relax – tempered only by the further few hours getting to Manchester. It was a shame she'd had to use the subterfuge of the business trip to Bahrain – she could, otherwise, have caught a direct flight rather than using the train as all the connecting flights from Heathrow to Manchester were full.

Once through passport control and customs, she caught the Heathrow Express to Paddington then the tube to Euston. In Dubai, her expenses were usually on the company credit card which she'd posted to Marshall, along with her letter of resignation, from Bahrain. She'd transferred most of her money to a new UK bank account and had arranged for new cards to be sent to the apartment before withdrawing all but a small balance from her local account.

Chapter 3.   Glen

Glen had completed a five thousand nautical mile journey, from the British Virgin Islands in the Caribbean to Chichester on the south coast of England, delivering a forty-three-foot Beneteau yacht back to the UK. The journey took just under six weeks, including a few days in the Azores and another sheltering in Falmouth while a deep low with its associated gale-force winds had driven up the channel. Had he been racing, he could have trimmed days off the time – but his priority was to minimise any strain on the yacht.

He'd taken the opportunity in Falmouth to clear his arrival in the UK with Border Control – and have a long bath in a hotel followed by a decent meal at a nearby restaurant.

Leaving the hotel lobby, he pulled up the collar of his yachting jacket against the rain. As he walked along the quayside, he reflected on the difference between the weather here and parts of the Australian outback where there would be months between any wets.

Once the low had passed, he set sail from Falmouth, catching the tide as it flooded up the Channel. The winds had moderated to a force five and was on his quarter driving him on at seven to eight knots. He watched the Eddystone lighthouse pass to his port as the yacht cut through the waves sending invigorating spray flying over the cockpit. Start Point Lighthouse, near Salcombe, was left astern as Glen prepared for his final night sail on this trip, thankful for the chance he'd had to rest in Falmouth. These were busy shipping lanes; he carried a radar reflector but its effectiveness depended on someone watching the radar and not all the bigger boats kept an adequate lookout.

As dawn broke, he was approaching St Catherine's point on the southern tip of the Isle of Wight. The light had acted as a guide for him for the last hour. The wind had now veered to the northwest and he hardened up his sails as he adjusted his course for Bembridge. Another two hours or so and he should be at the entrance to Chichester harbour; then up through the channel to the yacht basin. He checked his mobile and was glad to see that he had a signal and, as arranged, called the yacht's owner, Malcolm Lambert.

At the entrance to the harbour, he started the engine, furled the genoa and dropped the mainsail and motored up the restricted channel. The moorings were within a basin with lock gates to maintain the water level when the tides dropped and he'd been warned about the need to request entry clearance. As he approached the lock, another yacht was just leaving and he quickly received the green light to proceed.

Inside the basin, he identified the berth he'd been allocated. Standing on the pontoon was a couple dressed in matching sailing jackets. The man waved to Glen and gestured at the berth they were standing by. Glen acknowledged his signal, recognising the owner. He'd already positioned fenders along the side of the yacht and prepared mooring lines and he gently brought the boat alongside the pontoon. The couple separated; the woman approached the bow and Mr Lambert the stern. As the yacht squeezed the fenders against the pontoon, Glen put the engine out of gear, set the throttle to idle and passed the stern line to the owner; while he secured the line around a bollard, Glen made his way to the bow and passed another line to the woman.

"Good morning, Glen, how was your trip?" the owner asked.

"It was fine, thanks, Malcolm. Boat handled very well."

"Excellent, this is my wife, Patricia."

"Pleasure to meet you, Mrs Lambert," Glen said.

Having secured the yacht, Malcolm suggested that they go over to the yacht club for a drink.

"So, what are your plans now, Glen?" Patricia asked as her husband handed her a gin and tonic.

"I've got another commission in a couple of weeks taking a yacht from the Hamble down to Gibraltar. In the meantime, I'm going up to London for a few days then take a trip up to Lancashire where the family originally came from, see if I can dig up some information about our history."

"Sounds interesting, do you have any relations there?"

"Not that I know of. My great-grandparents emigrated to Oz just after the war, they were Ten-Pound Poms, so anyone from their generation is probably dead by now. There may be cousins around but I've never met any of them and don't have any contact details. But who knows what I might turn up?"

"So, you've never been to the UK before?"

"No, first time. Crazy really. I've been to plenty of other places around the world but never here before. I plan to have a look around London before heading north."

"Are you hiring a car to get around over here?" asked Patricia.

"Heck no. I've heard about the traffic, especially in London. I'm more used to driving in the outback. Two Ute's meeting each other counts as rush hour out there! I'm going to use the train and cabs. In fact, I'd better order one to get me to Chichester station."

"Don't worry about that, we can drop you off, can't we Malcolm?" Patricia suggested.

"Absolutely. It's on our way," her husband confirmed.

Chapter 4.   Jeff

Jeff's wife, Deborah, had taken their twin daughters, Charlotte and Jessica, to visit her parents for the weekend in Tonbridge so he planned to spend the weekend in Manchester as Yvette. He'd hoped to get away on the Friday but a problem at work had delayed his departure.

He'd spent the evening contemplating his situation and drinking several large single malts.

For years, he'd identified as a cross-dresser but, over the past three, perhaps four, years, he'd gradually concluded that he wasn't transvestite but transsexual – to use increasingly unpopular terms in the trans community; but how else did one differentiate between a male who wore female clothes and a female 'born in the wrong body'? There was a tendency now to refer to both as transgender; but it made no sense to say 'I used to be transgender; now I'm transgender'. No, for him, the obsolescent labels of transvestite and transsexual helped describe the change.

It wasn't that he was unsuccessful as a male. Far from it. He had a good job as a Senior Project and Programme Manager. Admittedly, the salary, good as it was, wouldn't have covered the mortgage on their four-bedroom detached house in the Surrey Hills outside Croydon if he hadn't inherited it from his parents when they were killed in a car accident. But it did allow the family to live comfortably, including paying for the girls to attend an expensive private school and own ponies that they kept, together with Deborah's horse, in livery stables ten minutes from the house. Jeff didn't ride. He preferred sailing, usually with a friend who kept a yacht on the Hamble.

Jeff could have taken his Audi TT to Manchester – but it was a very recognisable car and, potentially, a prime target for thieves in any inner-city area overnight. Far more relaxing to use public transport; especially as the South London tram line was only four hundred yards from their house giving easy access to East Croydon station and the fast trains to Victoria – then just four or five stops on the tube to Euston for the train to Manchester.

It was a very comfortable life. Whilst relations with Deborah weren't always smooth and he was sure she'd had a number of affairs with others in her riding and hunting set, he doted on the two girls and would do anything for them. No, that wasn't quite true. Try as he might; and he had, he couldn't stop being trans. That was part of him.

And, that was the problem. He couldn't carry on living as a male. But how could he transition? It would certainly cost him his job and that meant the end of their lifestyle. The girls would have to leave their school and give up their ponies and they'd never forgive him for that – let alone making them face the disgrace of having a transgender parent. Deborah would certainly condemn him and blame him for everything. She'd accuse him of making her a social outcast, unable to hold her head up amongst the horsey crowd. And, she'd be right. It would be his fault – she and the girls hadn't done anything to cause his problem. They were innocent victims of his condition.

He'd thought about taking his own life. But that wouldn't solve the financial problem. He had substantial insurance but it wouldn't pay out for suicide. He could just disappear – but, again, the insurance wouldn't pay out until he could be presumed dead – and that would take years. He'd considered employing someone to kill him and make it look like a mugging. But where did you find someone prepared to do that? What if they were caught and confessed to the conspiracy? There had to be a way out of his dilemma, but he couldn't see it. He poured himself another glass of whisky.

Chapter 5.   Euston

Nathan entered the platform as soon as the train was available to board. Pulling his suitcase behind him, he walked through the ticket barrier, praying that no one would ask to examine his luggage. Holmes had assured him that explosive sniffer dogs wouldn't be available for his train – though they'd certainly be on duty for the twenty past twelve service which a number of cabinet ministers would be on. He hadn't asked how Holmes knew this.

He glanced at the sleek rear coach of the Pendolino train and remembered that the original sets had been built just outside Birmingham but, like so much of English industry, that work had been moved overseas to foreigners. His seat was in the third coach, 'H'. He lifted his case onto the upper level of the luggage rack – ensuring that the explosion would be at head height causing maximum destruction rather than being absorbed by seat backs.

He then took his seat on the other side of the aisle with his back to the direction of travel so he could keep the case in full view.

Jeff was next to join the train. He'd put his problem over transition to the back of his mind as he anticipated spending the weekend in Manchester as Yvette, even if only for a few hours. Walking past coach H, he glanced in and wished he'd booked a first-class ticket rather than standard – but all the cheap deals had gone and he wasn't going to pay the full fare. Instead, his seat was near the front of Coach U.

He put his case on the rack just inside the door and took his seat by the window. Facing the rear of the train he saw Michelle walking along the platform pulling her small suitcase on wheels and carrying an airline cabin bag. She looked exactly how he'd like to be. Stylishly dressed, totally confident, her hair was fairly short –

his own was about the same length but hers was better groomed and highlighted. As far as he could see, she was mid-thirties, the same as him. She disappeared from view as she went past his window. He wondered where she'd come from and where she was going. Did the cabin bag suggest an overseas flight? If so, had it been a holiday or business? Her suitcase didn't look big enough for a holiday. So, maybe a short business trip? Paris, perhaps; or Rome? How he wished that could be him.

About fifteen yards behind Michelle was a guy carrying a sailing holdall and wearing a sailing jacket– Jeff recognised the Musto logo on both. Where had he come from? It wasn't likely he'd be using this service if he was on his way to a yachting trip. If he had been heading out of Liverpool or one of the North Wales ports – or somewhere further north, there were more direct routes. As he passed Jeff, the sailor switched his bag from one shoulder to the other, glanced into the coach then stopped – the back of his holdall just visible through the window. Then it disappeared too.

Jeff heard a thud from behind him as another passenger dropped their case into the luggage rack. Then the woman he'd seen coming up the platform stopped by his table and put her cabin bag on the window seat facing him. Michelle slid into the aisle seat then leaned back and closed her eyes. Jeff took out a copy of Project Management Today magazine and started to read an article he'd been meaning to finish for a few days. It couldn't hold his attention, however, so he put it down again and picked up a copy of Private Eye instead.

The flow of passengers joining the train and passing Jeff's seat stopped again as another newcomer dropped their bag on the luggage rack. As he took his place in the window seat across the aisle, Jeff saw that it was the sailor. Glen saw Jeff looking at him as he put his storm-proof jacket on the seat next to him. Jeff pretended to be looking through the window on that side; then their view of each other was blocked by a forty-something balding man heaving a suitcase along the aisle – bumping Michelle's seat as he struggled past.

"Sorry, love," he said, "the luggage rack's full at this end."

Michelle sat up, opened her cabin bag, took out her laptop and plugged it into the power socket under the window. Jeff was surprised to see that she didn't seem to enter any password as it booted up. But, maybe, she had no confidential material on it. Still, it wasn't good practice. Presumably she wasn't an IT professional.

Gradually the traffic down the aisle diminished as the remaining passengers joined the train and took their seats. The ones by Michelle, Jeff and Glen remained empty.

It was only when he saw items on the platform going past, that Jeff realised that the train had started moving. It soon picked up speed and headed out of Euston through the industrial areas north of the station. Other local and inter-city trains passed in the other direction, heading to the terminus, and, as it went faster and faster, it overtook other slab-fronted suburban services.

Michelle closed down her laptop and took a folder out of her bag. It was for a project management conference in Manchester. As she started to open the pack, she noticed Jeff looking at it. She was used to guys using any excuse to chat her up – but something told her that he might be different.

"Do you work in Project Management?" he asked, holding up his copy of PM Today.

"I do, are you attending the conference as well?" Michelle replied.

"Not this year," Jeff told her.

As the train headed north, they exchanged experiences and found they'd worked in similar fields. As Michelle's recent work had been in the Gulf States, they hadn't identified any mutual acquaintances.

"So, what are you working on at present?" Jeff asked.

"I'm just about to start a new project in Manchester. It's an unusual situation, I was interviewed online by the Project Director – it wasn't a good connection."

"Have you been to Manchester before?"

"Yes, for a visit, or passing through, never to stay for long. What about you?"

"Usually just on business; seeing suppliers and the like. Couple of times for test matches at Old Trafford. I had a look round the Lowry exhibition at Salford Quays."

"Really? The flat I've leased is near Salford Quays. Not sure how far it is from the Lowry Centre though. It's supposed to be close to the office I'll be working at. No doubt I'll find my way around before long."

"No friends or family in the area then?"

"No, I haven't had much chance to make friends in the UK with working abroad and I've lost touch with any I used to have. No family either. My parents were killed in a car crash last year. I couldn't even get back for the funeral due to Covid."

Chapter 6.   Stoke on Trent

The train pulled into Stoke on Trent station on time. The grubby brickwork of the station buildings apparently unchanged for more than half a century – stained by the smoke from decades of earlier steam trains, the exhaust from diesel engines and dust from the coal slag heaps that had dotted the area until the mining industry failed. Overhead a downpour thundered onto the canopy, leaking through in several places.

As it pulled out again, Michelle stood up, taking her handbag with her. Glen watched her as she walked the few steps to the toilet. As she closed the door behind her, he realised Jeff was watching him watching her.

"Nice looking woman, are you related?" he asked.

"No, we only met on the train."

"Oh, really? It's just that you looked so similar, same colour hair and eyes, similar facial structures, I wondered if you were twins. Sorry, you must think I'd been staring."

"Not at all. I noticed she was looking at a brochure for a business conference and realised we worked in similar jobs and just got comparing experiences."

"I see, so what line of work are you in?"

"IT Project Management. What about you?"

"I deliver yachts. Someone has a boat in one part of the world that they want somewhere else, they call me and I move it there for them."

"Interesting life."

"Can be. Sometimes too interesting if the weather blows up."

"Solitary life too, I should think."

"It is, but that suits me. No ties, just myself to look after."

"So, where's your next trip then?"

"Nothing for a couple of weeks – just completed a delivery from the British Virgin Islands to Chichester on the south coast. As you can guess from the accent, I'm from Oz but my grandparents were born near Manchester so I thought I'd take the opportunity to take a look at where they were from. I'm Glen by the way."

"My name's Jeff. So, do you have relations in the Manchester area?"

"Not that I know of. My parents died when I was young and I was brought up by my grandparents. We never talked about the old country or relations back here. Then the oldies passed away two years ago within a couple of months of each other."

In the next compartment, eight minutes after the train had left Stoke, Nathan stood up and, as instructed, left his coat and hat at his seat. Checking that he had his Stoke to Macclesfield ticket with him, he made his way to the luggage rack and opened the zip on the small pocket. He looked inside and checked the timer display indicated a ten-minute delay then moved a switch on the timer from safe to live.

He was proud to have been chosen to undertake this task. Proud that he'd evaded precautions at Euston – outsmarted the security services. He couldn't fail now. All he had to do was press the timer button then leave the train when it arrived at Macclesfield. It couldn't be easier.

The toilet door opened and Michelle started to come out. The train had picked up speed since leaving Stoke and was travelling through open country, with cows grazing in the fields, the carriages tilting as it went round bends.

Nathan's finger hovered over the start button; beads of sweat rolled down his forehead as he stabbed at the button detonating the explosives.

The bomb sprayed thousands of lethal bits of metal – ball bearings, nuts and bolts and screws – throughout the compartment to rip through exposed human bodies. The blast also lifted the front bogie of the coach off the rails dragging the next coach and the rear of the one containing Michelle, Glen and Jeff with it.

The coaches bumped and shook as the wheels bounced over the sleepers and ballast. Then the carriages started to tip on their sides as the momentum of the rear of the train continued to push the intervening coaches forward.

Jeff held on to the table and pressed his foot against the table leg. Behind him, Michelle was thrown to the side and fell into the seat facing Glen.

Automatic brakes caused the train wheels that were still on the track to screech as metal rubbed against metal but even that sound was soon drowned out by screams and crying and the sound of bodies being thrown around. With his back to the seat and braced against the table leg, Jeff was reasonably stable but he could see that Michelle was hurt. Glen was facing the direction of travel and had steadied himself against the table and the carriage wall. His experience of riding out rough weather on yachts had kicked in automatically. With luck, he might even escape with a few minor cuts and bruises.

But, his luck didn't hold out.

The carriage continued to tilt further and further and, just as it ended up on its side, it hit a concrete post that burst through the window next to Glen catching Michelle a blow to the head before smashing into Glen's face.

Eventually, the coach came to a stop.

Jeff took in the scene facing him. Glen was unrecognisable and Michelle's head lolled to one side. Blood trickling down his own face told him he'd been hit himself by something flying through the broken window – but it didn't feel serious. At least all his limbs seemed to be intact. He was surprised to note that his breathing and heart rates appeared normal; he seemed to be viewing the situation as though it was a dream and not happening to him. He gingerly lowered himself down to the others and confirmed that both were dead. There was nothing that anyone could do for either of them – two individuals with no one to miss them or mourn for them.

He then realised that this presented him with an opportunity. It wasn't as though he was hurting anyone. It was, he rationalised, like organ donation – allowing someone else to live when you were gone. Only, instead of body parts, he would take their identities and leave his in the train wreck. It would free his family of the trauma and disgrace of transition. The insurance could hardly refuse to pay out for a terrorist attack; in fact, the payout would be higher for accidental death.

Jeff looked around the coach – everyone was completely absorbed in their own problems and no one was taking any notice of him. He took his wallet and mobile and swopped them for Glen's and slid his watch and wedding and signet rings onto Glen's wrist and fingers. Michelle's cabin bag had fallen next to where she lay against the remains of the window. His own suitcase was still in the luggage rack. He opened the front pocket and took out the handbag he used when out as Yvette; it contained a purse with a debit card for an account he'd set up in Yvette's name and the 'pay as you go' mobile he used while en femme; he exchanged them for Michelle's handbag which he put in her cabin bag. He also took Glen's holdall from the luggage rack and his jacket.

He crawled along what had been the side of seats and the toilet to the door between the coaches. He could see that the train had broken in two at this point – the next coach was still upright and half on the rails about thirty yards away. The connecting door was missing giving only a few feet drop to the ground below. He paused to catch his breath.

"Are you OK mate?" someone called.

There were several figures half running half walking along the side of the front half of the train. Others were making their way down the embankment getting as far from the accident as they could. Sitting on the edge of where the door had been, Jeff jumped out of the train.

"Any help needed in there, mate? Anyone hurt?" asked a male wearing the train company's uniform. "Do you know what happened?"

"I think there was an explosion in one of the coaches behind ours then all hell broke loose as we left the track and tipped over. There're two dead just inside the coach and plenty of others hurt further down the carriage."

"Shit, OK, pal, you just take it easy. Help is on its way."

Chapter 7.   Aftermath

The crash scene was in open country just over a mile south of Congleton. The train manager called for assistance as soon as the train stopped and she was able to assess the situation. The initial call contained no details – only that the 10.20 from Euston had crashed and there were almost certainly casualties. Within minutes, passengers in the first-class coaches who had not been killed started to call 999 or 112.

A Major Emergency was declared and ambulances, fire service and police were directed to the scene. the derailed carriages stretched for several hundred yards and multiple teams trudged across the fields from the road through various gaps in the hedges.

The first to reach the carriage that Jeff had been in arrived two or three minutes after he'd climbed out. A cursory examination by a para-medic established that Jeff had no life-threatening injuries so, after giving him a blanket to keep him warm, he moved on to deal with the more seriously injured. Jeff could see the flashing blue lights on the road two hundred yards away.

As he slogged his way to the road, more and more emergency services personnel and other volunteers arrived and he was asked several times if he needed any help. One insisted on carrying the sailing holdall and Michelle's briefcase for him.

"Thanks, I'm fine now," he told his helper when they reached the road.

A female police officer took his arm.

"Come and sit down, m'duck, there should be a hot drink soon. We've also asked for transport – though goodness knows how long it will take to arrive."

She led him into a barn where he sat down on a straw bale. She then hurried away to help the next casualty.

As he sat there, he could see more volunteers arriving with a range of items they hoped would help. Some erected gazebos to provide some shelter; others set up gas cookers and picnic tables to prepare and serve hot drinks, yet others arrived with camping chairs. Someone even set up a toilet tent complete with Portaloo.

The barn quickly filled up with the walking wounded and uninjured passengers off the train. Jeff took the opportunity to check the documents he'd taken from Glen – including his passport, driving licence, and credit cards. The wallet contained less money than he'd had in his own wallet – but that would be a small price to pay for a new identity that allowed him to make a fresh start.

The roads near the crash site were narrow lanes and rapidly became congested with emergency services competing to get as close as possible. Fire and Rescue drove across the fields to get their recovery equipment as close as possible to the derailed coaches.

Overhead, air ambulances from the West Midlands and North West started to approach the site ready to evacuate the most seriously injured casualties who might still be saved.

Approaching through the fields, members of a local golf club were arriving in their 4x4s, their off-road abilities finally of use. They could ferry some of the uninjured to the clubhouse to await onward transportation.

Jeff gratefully accepted their offer and, together with four others, climbed aboard a Mercedes GLS after putting his holdall and cabin bag in the luggage compartment. A few minutes later, he was being directed into the club reception. Three police officers were setting up a table near the entrance to the bar.

"Can you bear with us please, gentlemen? We just need to identify everyone from the incident and take brief statements and contact details from you."

Jeff wondered if this was where his plans would hit the buffers – the metaphor seemed appropriate under the circumstances. But he needn't have worried. He was asked to give his name and provide identification.

One of Jeff's party tricks was as an impressionist; he could mimic almost anyone, male or female. He had never suffered from the usual problem of his voice giving him away when dressed. He could be Margo from The Good Life, Dot Cotton from EastEnders or any one of a dozen other TV characters. Imitating Michelle would be no problem; but when giving his details to the police, he adopted his Paul Hogan impression.

If the officer had looked more closely, he might have wondered about the photograph but he only gave it a cursory glance. His shift had been about to end when he was ordered to get in a minibus and assist at the incident. He was well aware that he'd be lucky to finish before late evening – putting the kybosh on his plans for a date with the new probationer at the station.

"So, Mr Hargreaves, can you tell me what happened from your perspective?"

"I can't tell you very much. We'd left Stoke station and there was suddenly this explosion from one of the carriages behind us. The train then derailed and we ended up on the side. The guy across the aisle was hit when something smashed into his face. A woman had just come out of the toilet and was thrown around.

Once the train stopped, I climbed down to them to see if there was anything I could do – but they were both dead."

"I see, do you happen to know their names?"

"I think the guy introduced himself as Jeff something. Oh, maybe I should mention, when I got on the train, Jeff was sitting in the seat I was supposed to have. He apologised and offered to move but said he preferred to face forwards and he'd been allocated one with his back to the engine. I didn't care, in fact, I was very happy to swop as it gave me a chance to chat to a woman sitting at the same table. Turned out to be a very lucky move for me."

"Certainly was, Sir. Do you know what happened to the woman sitting opposite you?"

"Sorry, no. She stood up as we left Stoke – I assumed she was going to the buffet car or the toilet. Her name was Michelle, though. I didn't get her surname."

"Thanks Mr Hargreaves. Hopefully she was in one of the other coaches and came to no harm. I think that's all we need from you but we've got your phone number if we need to be in touch. Now, if you could just check and sign the statement."

Confident that any discrepancy in his signature would be accounted for by the shock of the day's events, Jeff went up to the bar. He ordered a lager and took it across to a table. He had nearly finished drinking it when a man wearing the train company's uniform entered.

"Could I have your attention please?"

The room fell silent.

"We are arranging buses to take you to Macclesfield, where a train will take you on to Stockport and Manchester Piccadilly. The first should be here in about ten minutes. Thank you."

A queue quickly gathered outside the ladies' toilet as passengers 'of a certain age' prepared themselves for an unpredictable journey.

Chapter 8.   Manchester

It was another two hours before Jeff finally reached Manchester Piccadilly. On the concourse, Jeff took stock. He'd already booked and paid for a room as Yvette – but she needed to have died in the train crash to allow him to use Michelle's identity. He needed to find an inexpensive hotel. As he didn't know Glen's PINs, he'd have to pay by cash or keep the amount below the contactless limit. He bought a coffee from one of the concessions and found a seat.

Using Glen's phone, he searched for budget hotels in the area and found one claiming to be just five minutes from the station. He was able to book it online using Glen's payment card which made life easier.

Having reserved a room for three nights, he hitched his holdall over his shoulder, picked up Michelle's bag and strode out of the station following the map link.

The receptionist checked the booking then handed him his key.

"Do you want me to take a credit card pre-authorisation in case you want to charge anything to the room?" she asked.

"No thanks, I'll probably go out for a meal later."

"That's fine, Mr Hargreaves. Enjoy your stay."

In his room, Jeff tossed the holdall onto the bed and made himself a cup of coffee.

He opened Michelle's carry-on bag and examined the contents. Taking her handbag out first, he unzipped the main compartment; it contained the usual: a purse with about fifty pounds in cash but, surprisingly, no debit or credit cards; a passport and the remains of airline tickets from Bahrain to Heathrow.

There was also a letter from her bank that confirmed arrangements to transfer her funds from a local account in the Gulf to a new account in the UK. It advised that her new cards and PIN details would be sent to the apartment to await her arrival. He put the letter to one side along with her driving licence.

In a separate zipped pocket, he found a thick envelope. Opening it, he discovered it contained £30,000 in fifty-pound notes.

"Shit," he thought. "I wonder how she came by that." Perhaps working in the Middle East paid even better than he'd thought!

The cabin bag held the laptop Jeff had seen Michelle use on the train and two large envelopes. The first contained details of the job she'd spoken about; the other a rental agreement for the apartment in the Quays. The bag also held a nightdress and underwear, wash kit and make-up bag.

Jeff switched on the laptop. It opened up without requiring a passcode – which surprised him, but was a relief. He searched her data files and found folders for the new job and the apartment. Michelle was clearly very well organised as the folder about the job included the original details, her application and covering letter, questions she planned to ask; and a file about the organisation she'd be working for. She'd even recorded the Zoom session of the interview. Jeff could see that the connection had been unreliable; the video cut out frequently and the sound quality was poor. The image was barely recognisable as Michelle.

She was due to start work in a week's time on the Monday – which was just as well as Jeff would have plenty to do in the meantime.

He transferred the remaining cash from Michelle's purse into Glen's wallet, put Michelle's handbag into the room safe and set the combination, then left the room. He walked up to Piccadilly Gardens and found an Italian Restaurant for dinner. As he ate his Tagliatelle and drank his Pinot Grigio, he wondered if this really was a dream come true. Could he actually adopt Michelle's identity – and get away with it?

How would his family react to the news of his 'death'? He suspected Deborah's initial thoughts would be around financial matters. She knew he was well-insured and wasn't likely to wait long before making a claim; probably as soon as his body had been identified. Hopefully his own statement to the police – and the documents he'd planted on the body – would mean that she'd only have to identify his wedding ring and watch. Why would anyone want to dig deeper when there were so many other victims? The girls would probably miss him – but, then, if he'd transitioned as Jeff, they'd have lost their dad in any case. Like most kids, he was sure they'd eventually get over him.

Tomorrow, he'd have to go shopping. He had no female clothing any longer. Everything had been abandoned along with Yvette. He'd seen from Michelle's dossier that she'd shipped most of her belongings back to the UK and they'd arrive in a few days. He doubted, however, that many of her things would fit him – she'd looked about his height of five foot seven but was slimmer. He guessed she'd be a size ten or twelve while he was a fourteen.

He took out Glen's phone to see what news there was about the crash. The wallpaper showed a racing yacht. He recognised it as the 1983 Australian America's Cup winner Australia II skippered by John Bertrand. Then a thought struck him. Glen couldn't have used combinations of 1983 and II as his PIN, could he?

On his way back to the hotel, Jeff tested his theory at an ATM. '1183' was rejected but '8311' gave him access to Glen's account. He checked the balance – a little over three thousand Australian dollars. He tried withdrawing two hundred pounds and was rewarded.

In his room, he switched the television to a 24-hour news channel which was focussing on the crash.

"The explosion, which killed twenty-nine passengers and injured more than a hundred others, thirty-nine of them seriously, is believed to have been caused by a terrorist of Middle Eastern heritage. Twelve of the injured were air-lifted to hospitals in Stoke on Trent and Manchester. At least three of these have life-changing injuries. Most of the dead and seriously injured victims were in the first-class coach which was the site of the explosion. A number were believed to be attending the Conservative Party Conference including several local party executive members. The Prime Minister paid tribute to the hard work that constituency committees did for the party and sent his condolences to the families of those who had been killed or injured. Peter Holmes, leader of Action for England, condemned the attack as a cowardly deed and said it showed the need to repatriate all those who posed a threat to civilisation," intoned the newsreader.

Jeff poured himself a glass of wine then sat on the bed with a notepad and started to list what he had to do and what he needed to buy.

He started with clothes for work – dresses, skirts and blouses, shoes, handbag, jewellery, make-up, perfume and the rest. The clothes needed to fit well and look good so he definitely needed to try them on, but using changing rooms while dressed as male would attract unwanted attention.

The option was to buy a few basics like jeans and sweatshirts and a pair of trainers and some cosmetics as Michelle's were not the right shades. He could then return to the hotel to change and do his make-up and hair. His appearance would then be sufficiently feminine to avoid questions when trying on other clothes and shoes and buying more underwear. Later, he'd get his ears pierced and his hair done and, perhaps his nails.

Once he could appear convincingly as Michelle, he could move into the apartment and arrange delivery of her shipment from Dubai. He'd also need to stock the flat with food and buy any household items he might need. He had to stop thinking of himself as 'he'; Jeff was no more. *SHE* was now Michelle – with occasional forays, at present, as Glen.

As the next morning was Sunday, the shops Michelle needed opened late so she had a long soak in the bath and ate a leisurely breakfast before leaving the hotel for the shopping area. She found the trainers and socks, jogging trousers, sweatshirt and a padded jacket she wanted in one of the sportswear shops and tights in Wilko. Stage One completed, Michelle returned to the hotel where she got changed and applied her make-up.

It was unlikely that the hotel staff would notice her leaving and, if they did, the chances of them realising that 'Michelle' was not registered as a guest were slim. They weren't likely to care in any case, but it still gave her a nervous thrill as she paced across the foyer from the lift to the exit.

Back in the Arndale Centre, Michelle's next objective was to find some smart shoes. That task completed with a pair of black two-inch heel court shoes, she could move her look up a notch from casual to smart with a dress or skirt and blouse – or two. She kept one of the dresses on in place of the jogging trousers and sweatshirt and wore the high heels when she left the shop. Any androgynous look had now been eliminated and she swung her hips, the skirt brushing her legs deliciously, as she made her way to another store. She was undecided whether to choose Marks and

Spencer's or Next for underwear, nightdresses and more dresses or skirts and tops that she wanted. Not that it mattered, she'd be visiting the other before long to add to her wardrobe. On this occasion, Next won.

By now, her purchases were becoming too much to carry so she bought a wheeled suitcase and put the bags inside. She then crossed the road to Boots for the other make-up, skincare and other bits and pieces she needed. She filled a basket with boxes of tissues, cotton buds and pads, hair brushes and combs and a hair dryer and styling brush.

"The airline lost my bag so all I had left was my touch-up kit," she explained to the beautician on one of the counters. "But, in any case, it's probably time for me to update my look, what would you advise?"

The beautician glanced at the overflowing basket and quickly realised that this would be a lucrative sale – and spent the next hour demonstrating her products and making up Michelle's face, giving suggestions for different looks for day and evening.

One purchase she hadn't been able to make was to replace the fillers she used in her bras as Yvette.

After years of experimenting with different ideas from rolled-up socks, through large balloons filled with jelly or birdseed, she'd finally purchased a pair of prostheses from a specialist shop. They'd been expensive but she'd had to abandon them with her other female attire. Back at the hotel, she booted up Michelle's laptop and searched for replacements. She found some on Amazon and, whilst reluctant to use them for anything but essentials, placed an order to be delivered to one of their lockers.

Chapter 9.   Manchester: Monday

Next morning, she dressed as Michelle and took the tram out to the Harbour City stop – literally on the apartment block's doorstep. She went into the lettings office and produced their letters and provided Michelle's passport as identification – hoping, desperately, that Tanya, the administrator, wouldn't look closely at the photograph. As expected, the letter was sufficient evidence of Michelle's right to the property and the passport was returned after a cursory glance.

"There's your welcome pack, Ms Hartley. If you'd like to come with me, I'll take you up."

Michelle pulled her case behind her as Tanya led the way.

"Post is delivered to the mailboxes over there," she told Michelle. "The key is in your welcome pack. Did you want to check if there is anything for you now?"

Michelle identified her box and opened it; there were several letters which she put into her airline bag while Tanya walked over to the lifts.

"Your key card gives you access to the main door after office hours and the lifts, and to the gym through those double doors," Tanya said as she tapped one against the call button. "Please ensure you and any guests you give cards to take care of them. There is a charge for replacements."

Tanya stood aside to let Michelle enter the lift.

The ride up was smooth and the lift quickly reached Michelle's floor. The 12th-floor flat was on the north-western corner of the block. The front door led into a hall with two bedrooms, bathroom, lounge and kitchen leading off the central corridor.

As advertised, the apartment was well furnished – beds and wardrobes and seating in the lounge; the kitchen was fitted out with a cooker, fridge-freezer, washing machine and a kettle. The cupboards contained a few mugs and other crockery. Michelle realised she'd need to work out what else she needed.

"There're some tea bags, coffee, it's only instant I'm afraid, sugar and some long-life milk. Most new residents welcome a cuppa when they move in," Tanya smiled. "There's a Sainsbury's local nearby for other shopping you might want – and the usual larger supermarkets around the area; the details are in the welcome pack."

"That's great. Everything looks fine. I think I'll make myself a drink. Would you like one?" Michelle asked.

"Thanks, but I need to get back to the office. You have our number if you need anything. I hope you have a great time living here." Tanya replied before letting herself out of the flat.

Michelle rinsed the kettle out then refilled it. While it boiled, she looked out of the kitchen window at the distant hills and the tiny figures of wind turbines on the moorland. Hearing the kettle click off she poured the water into a mug containing instant coffee which she then took into the lounge.

She opened the large bulky envelope first that must have been hand-delivered as there were no stamps on it. A set of keys fell out of it as she did so.

Inside, she found a letter from the company welcoming her and outlining the induction programme for the following Monday. It also told her that her company car was in the basement garage and gave the registration number. The letter confirmed that she was permitted to use it for private trips as well as business.

The next envelopes she opened were from Michelle's bank and contained debit and credit cards. Two further envelopes contained the PINs for the two cards. The credit card had a limit of £20,000. The next envelope she opened contained a deposit account bank statement and, when she saw the balance, she nearly spat out her coffee. It was for a little over £165,000. Another identical envelope contained a current account statement with a balance of just under £15,000.

Michelle had known overseas contracts could be lucrative with most of the day-to-day expenses covered – leaving the salary to accumulate – but more than two hundred thousand pounds? Then she remembered that Michelle had mentioned that her parents had been killed in a car accident. No doubt some of the funds had been from their estate.

The last letter was from the shipping company asking her to contact them on arrival so they could arrange delivery of her consignment from Dubai. She dealt with that immediately and arranged for it to arrive the next day.

Michelle then started to list what she would need for the flat. Having done so, she took the lift down to the basement garage. In the space allocated to her flat sat a red Audi A3 – which matched the information in the letter. She clicked the remote control and the hazard lights flashed as the central locking activated. She pulled open the driver's door and slid into the seat. Adjusting the position and familiarising herself with the controls, she drank in the new car aroma.

Satisfied that she knew where things were, and having programmed the sat nav for the Trafford Centre, she started the engine, backed out of the space and drove out of the garage. Within fifteen minutes, she was parking outside John Lewis' which she thought most likely to have all the items she would need.

Two hours later, she'd visited the bedding department (where she'd spent more than she ever imagined she would on sumptuous duvet covers, pillowcases and sheets), then the kitchen and dining departments and bought everything on her list, including a coffee machine – no more instant coffee – and several items she'd overlooked. They would be taken to the pick-up point for her while she had some lunch.

A text from Amazon, while she was having lunch, advised that her order had been left in a locker at Salford City shopping centre so she called in on the way home. Much of the remainder of the afternoon was spent unpacking everything and putting it away in the apartment. While taking a break and making a coffee with her new machine she realised that she still needed to stock up on other groceries. There was a small 'local' store under a nearby tower block, but she wanted a wider range to choose from so drove to the main supermarket about a mile away.

By the time she finished shopping and stowing everything in the cupboards, in spite of the well-stocked fridge, she decided to go out to one of the restaurants around Media City to eat. Over dinner, she checked for news of the attack on the train. Few of the victims had been named as their next of kin needed to be notified first. She wondered how her own family would react to the news and felt guilty about the pain she was putting them through but knew she wouldn't have been able to continue living as Jeff.

Either of the other options, taking her own life or transitioning as Jeff would have caused just as much grief, perhaps even more, for Deborah, Charlotte and Jessica. This way, they'd be financially secure and without the embarrassment of being related to a tranny.

Of course, she'd miss the two girls. But what else could she have done? It wasn't their fault that she was trans. Nor was it her fault.

She hadn't asked to be that way. In truth, the problem wasn't hers, it was how society, or, at least, a significant section of it, regarded trans people.

Michelle finished her meal then asked for the bill, adding a decent tip to the charge. Would the waitress actually receive the extra, she wondered? That was one of the problems with the insistence on contactless payments due to Covid.

She pulled her coat around her and slipped her handbag over her shoulder as she left the restaurant to make her way back to the apartment. Chilly winds were gusting round the brightly lit blocks surrounding the piazza. A tram was pulling out of the Media City stop, rattling over the points on its way into the city centre. A show must have just finished at the Lowry Theatre as the tram was full and crowds were filtering onto the platform to wait for the next service.

Back at the flat, she poured herself a glass of wine, took it into the lounge and stared out of the window over Media City and the Lowry Centre. A dark ribbon showed where the Manchester Ship Canal made its way to Liverpool. Did any ships still use it, apart from leisure craft? she wondered. Off to the south, she could see the flashing beacons of aircraft on their final approach to Manchester Airport.

She drained the last of the wine then cleansed and toned her face and undressed for bed. She put on her long silky nightdress, luxuriating in the sensual feel of the material against her skin.

Lying in bed, she mentally ran over what she still needed to do.

Her first priority was to check Glen out of the hotel near Piccadilly Station. That had to be done in male mode; hopefully the last time she'd ever have to present in that way. The rest of her life would be spent as Michelle, although she might still need Glen's identity as background when she saw a Gender Identity Specialist for a referral for surgery. She also wondered whether to respond to the police request for anyone on the train to contact them so they could be eliminated from enquiries regarding unidentified bodies. She decided to call them in the morning.

Chapter 10. Surrey Hills: Monday

DC Vicky Porter hated this part of the job, informing someone that their husband might be dead. In this case, the victim had been badly mutilated in the train explosion near Manchester.

There had, however, been substantial evidence suggesting that the individual was Jeffrey Shaw. Forensics had found identification, including a driving licence, credit cards and a phone registered to the same person. They had also been wearing signet and wedding rings and a Rolex watch.

She parked on the street outside the address and walked up the drive to the front door. There was a Range Rover parked in front of one of the up-and-over garage doors. Ringing the bell, she took a step back.

A tall woman in her late thirties, her blonde hair tied up in a ponytail, opened the door.

"Yes?"

"Mrs Shaw?"

"Yes, but whatever it is I'm not buying."

Vicky showed her Warrant Card.

"Mrs Shaw, I'm Detective Constable Porter, may I come in and have a word? It's about your husband."

"He's not here."

"Do you know where he is? Has he been in touch in the last few days?"

"Not since Friday, he's away at the moment and my daughters and I were visiting my parents in Sussex. Why? What's this about?"

"If I could just come in for a minute?"

Deborah Shaw sighed in frustration.

"If you must. Come through to the sitting room."

She pointed to the sofa.

"Sit down, please. Now what is this about?" she asked as she sat down, taking a cigarette and lighting it.

"Mrs Shaw, could you please look at these photographs and tell me if you recognise what you see."

Vicky passed her pictures of the rings, watch and jacket.

"I can't be certain about the jacket but Jeff has a similar one. The rings are his though and the watch is the same as his. I could check the serial number if that helps – it's recorded for the insurance. Why? What's going on? Why do you have these photographs?"

"The serial number would help, thank you. And do you know what else he was wearing on Saturday by any chance?"

"No idea. As I said, we went to my parents on Friday so we weren't here on Saturday. What's this about?"

"Have you any idea why he was going to Manchester?"

"He said something about a Project Management conference he might attend – other than that, I have no idea. Why? Tell me what this is all about."

"I'm afraid it's likely that he was involved in the train explosion near Manchester."

"What do you mean 'involved'? Has he been hurt? Where is he?"

"I'm sorry to say we have reason to believe that your husband was killed in the incident."

Vicky thought she saw Deborah's eyes widen and a twitch of the corners of her lips before she put her hand to her mouth and the gesture was hidden.

"The watch and rings were found on a body in a seat that we believe he had reserved. There was also a wallet containing identification and a mobile phone registered to him on the body. I'm so sorry to bring you this news. Is there anyone I can call to come and be with you?" she continued.

"Are you certain that it's him? Don't you have photographs of him?"

"Unfortunately, his face was damaged beyond recognition – which is why we're having to use belongings found on the body. There's no record on our system of his fingerprints or DNA. But, no, I don't think there is any doubt."

Deborah Shaw stubbed out her cigarette.

"Is it possible that someone stole his property and was wearing it?"

"It's not impossible, but we don't think that's at all likely. Thieves would normally sell their ill-gotten gains rather than use them, especially expensive watches and mobiles. We could try matching DNA samples with any known body samples from your husband if you want, perhaps from a hairbrush, bedding or the headrest in his car; we could even compare his DNA with your children's. To be honest familial DNA wouldn't be conclusive unless it showed no match at all. In any case, under the circumstances, I don't think there can be any doubt now you've identified the items. If the victim had been a thief, it's very likely we'd have their fingerprints on file and, as I said, we don't." Vicky replied as gently as she could.

"I see," she said, her eyes flicking from side to side for a moment before she seemed to recover her composure. "Thank you. What happens now?"

"It would be helpful if you could make a written statement and attend the Coroner's Court to provide formal identification."

Deborah's face was stiff-lipped as she got out of her chair.

"Of course. You'll let me know when I'm needed?"

"Certainly," Vicky replied as she stood up and left the room.

Deborah watched Vicky walk back to her car and drive off then picked up her mobile. Her call went through to voicemail.

"Oliver, it's me. Call me back as soon as you can."

Reporting to her boss when she returned to the office, Vicky gave him her impressions.

"She was a cold fish, hardly displayed any emotion. If the explosion hadn't happened three hundred miles from where she was, she might have been on my list of suspects," Vicky told him.

"Well, grief strikes people in different ways," he replied.

"Maybe. I'm glad that job's over for us though."

"True, at least we've helped to clear up the identification of one of the victims. Still twenty-odd to go I believe."

Deborah's phone rang as she was drinking a gin and tonic. She checked the display and answered.

"Oliver, the police have been here. They're saying that Jeffrey was caught up in that train explosion at the weekend. He's dead."

She'd met Oliver Matthews at Hickstead, where the girls had been competing in a Pony Club competition. His own horse had been injured so he wasn't taking part himself.

"Dead? My God. That's awful. I know he was an idiot – but even so. Are they sure it's him?"

"Well, it seems his face was damaged beyond recognition but they found a body wearing his rings and watch and with his wallet on him."

"Can't they do one of those DNA tests to be certain?"

"They need samples from him to compare. They suggested from his pillow or the bed headrest but I didn't think it would be helpful for you to have to provide a sample for elimination."

"Ah, no. That wouldn't be convenient. Would it?"

"No, darling, it wouldn't. His death is convenient though. It means I'm free of him without having to split everything in a divorce."

"They also said they could compare the DNA with the girls' but, well, I'm not sure there would be any family link to find and I really don't want them discovering that Jeffrey wasn't their father."

"Yes, I see your point. How are the girls taking it?"

"I haven't told them yet, Oliver. I need to go and get them from school. They'll be upset, of course, but they'll get over it. People do and life does have to go on. Maybe a new pony each will help distract them. Now, look, we'll have to keep a low profile until this blows over, darling."

Chapter 11. Manchester: Tuesday

The next morning, dressed in the jeans, trainers and padded jacket she'd worn when registering at the hotel as Glen, Michelle caught the tram from Harbour City. It was already packed with commuters heading to work in the city centre. The track wound between the buildings surrounding the old Salford Docks, criss-crossing roads and going up and down ramps and over stretches of water before climbing and running on the elevated section between the River Irwell and Chester Road – then dropping down again to street level at St Peter's Square. Alighting at Piccadilly Station, Michelle was soon at the hotel. Having collected the last of his luggage from the room, Michelle checked out, using Glen's debit card to pay for the wine he'd had from the mini-bar on her first night.

Half an hour later, Michelle was back in the apartment to shower and change.

Opening Glen's sailing bag, she removed any documents that might be needed; put underwear and toiletries to one side for disposal and repacked the rest of Glen's clothes. They could go to a charity shop. If anyone asked, *'they'd been left by an ex-boyfriend'* would be a credible excuse.

As she discarded male clothes for the last time, putting them in a black bin liner to be ceremonially disposed of, she wondered where her new life would take her.

Michelle and Jeff's careers had been very similar so she was well qualified and had the experience to cover her new role and had no qualms about work. But what about the rest of her life? Would she end up in a relationship? If so, would it be with a man or a woman? Her previous relationships had been with women but, even then, she'd often thought about how it would have been to be the other person in the relationship.

Obviously, she'd have to have surgery before having sex as a female.

For that, Michelle would have to register with a gender specialist. The international guidelines required a year living in role before surgery. There was ample evidence of Michelle having existed for a lot longer but that might demand explanations about why she hadn't sought hormones earlier let alone surgery. It would probably be safer to pretend that she'd only recently started living as Michelle – effectively merging Glen and Michelle's backgrounds. She might not have Glen's years of blue water practice from delivering yachts around the world but she had sufficient experience of sailing to talk knowledgeably, if ever required, on the subject. Jeff had participated in numerous Round the Island and cross channel races, two Fastnets and a RORC Transatlantic race from Lanzarote to Grenada. The chance of meeting anyone who'd encountered Glen was virtually non-existent – his work had involved spending more than 90% of his time on his own in the middle of oceans.

She went online and searched for UK-based services that might help her and, having compared the options, registered with one of them. Answering the pages of questions they asked, she was glad to have Glen's background as well as Michelle's to draw on, as using Michelle's only would have highlighted some discrepancies in her story.

At the end of the registration process, she booked an initial consultation for one evening the following week. The website warned to allow four weeks before treatment started. That wasn't too bad, though she was keen to start hormones as soon as possible. If it proved much longer, there was always the option of ordering them through the internet. In the meantime, she could organise any blood tests that might be needed and register with an NHS GP.

She made a cup of coffee, savouring the aroma, while she searched for hair salons in the area and made an appointment for 'the works' – hair, nails, waxing, eyebrows and fake tan – for the next morning, taking advantage of a cancellation. As she finished her call to the salon, her phone rang.

It was the security desk advising that her Dubai shipment had arrived. She spent the next couple of hours unpacking and sorting through the consignment. Apart from several designer handbags, other accessories and clothes, most of which were, as she'd anticipated, a size too small, ornaments and paintings, there were some books, CDs and DVDs, including some she knew weren't available on Netflix. At first glance, there seemed to be quite an overlap of taste in music and films. The only problem was that the apartment didn't have a system on which to play them – she needed to do some more shopping.

She drove back to John Lewis' and found an assistant in the television department who was only too willing to advise on a suitable system. An hour later, she entered her PIN to authorise over five thousand pounds for the purchase of a Smart, wall mounted, television, digital recorder and hi-fi system which would be installed by the end of the week. She then bought shelving from the furniture department to hold her books, the DVDs and some of the CDs – the rest she'd probably digitise and transfer to an MP3 player.

She spent the next two hours wandering around the Trafford Centre, identifying where she would be most likely to find suitable outfits to wear for work.

As male, Jeff had tended to wear suits when attending formal meetings but dressed slightly more casually when working in the office – typically a sports jacket or blazer with slacks. Although Michelle wouldn't be able to wear her predecessor's outfits or shoes, she could use most of her accessories including the designer handbags, scarves and some fabulous jewellery. Replacing the rest of her wardrobe would be fun.

Having made her way around both levels of the Trafford Centre, she called into Marks and Spencer's to stock up on basic lingerie; leaving with three large carrier bags full; two of underwear and another of food.

Back at the flat, she relaxed with a large glass of Chardonnay while standing at the lounge window and looking out at the view over Media City and the Lowry Centre. Looking to her left, she could see the floodlights at Manchester United's ground about half a mile or so away.

The cooker timer announced that a lasagne she'd put in the oven was ready so she put her empty glass on the dining table and served dinner.

Chapter 12. Wednesday: Point of No Return

The following morning, Michelle dressed casually for her appointment at the hairdressers.

This was a point of no return.

Until now, she could walk away from Michelle's life and reappear as Jeff – perhaps pleading loss of memory to explain his absence over the last four days. There might be some questions to explain away – such as how did his watch, ring and wallet end up on another person's body. But he could simply plead ignorance.

Once Michelle had been to the salon and had her hair coloured and restyled, eyebrows tidied, legs waxed, fake tan and nail extensions done, explanations would be impossible.

But it's what she'd dreamed of for years and there was no going back. There'd never be another opportunity like this to transition.

She slipped on her jacket, picked up her handbag and keys and took the lift to the basement car park. It was a crisp morning as she drove the short distance to the salon.

The experience was totally different to going to a barber. As Jeff, it would have been 'usual trim, mate?' and cost ten pounds. Today's visit wasn't likely to leave much change from two hundred pounds, perhaps more, even without allowing for tips. But, then, she was having a great deal more done. Jeff's usual trim would take twenty minutes; Michelle's highlights, colour, wash, trim and style would take over two hours – then there were the other treatments.

In fact, it was nearly four and a half hours later before Michelle was admiring the results in the mirror. It had been worth the pain of waxing and plucking.

"Absolutely wonderful," she gushed. The highlights made her hair look as though it had been bleached in the desert sun and matched the spray tan. Her eyebrows were perfect and her legs felt silky smooth. No one would doubt now that she'd just returned from the Middle East. The new style was also sufficiently different to Michelle's to account for any variation in appearance since her Zoom interview. The rest would be explained by the poor video and audio links.

Over the next few days, she shopped for clothes for work, for casual and for evenings out (if she ever got the opportunity); supervised the installation of her home entertainment system and sorted out the books, DVDs and CDs and stored them on the bookcases. She also researched her new employers on the internet and information on systems similar to the one she'd be working on.

Chapter 13. Initiation

Michelle had set her alarm for six o'clock to allow plenty of time to get ready for the first day at her new job. This could be make or break day. Michelle had to be one hundred per cent convincing in role or she was in deep trouble.

She'd taken care to select the perfect outfit: a geometric patterned sleeveless, boat-necked dress in navy and white, a pair of Jimmy Choo court shoes with six-centimetre heels found in Selfridges and a Saint Laurent shoulder bag – part of the consignment shipped back from Dubai. A knee-length coat to wear over the top completed the ensemble.

After showering, and a coffee and a bowl of cereal for breakfast, she dressed and did her make-up. Pausing at the flat door, Michelle closed her eyes for a moment and took a deep breath. Letting it out, she determinedly opened the door, locked it behind her and strode to the lift, her heels clicking on the tiled floor.

As the office was only a few hundred yards from the flat, there was no point using the car, it would take longer to drive and park again than to walk. Besides, it was a pleasant morning and the stroll would be good exercise.

Her office was on the sixth floor in one of the glass towers that had sprung up around the Quays. The company ID badge allowed her to pass through the security barrier at the entrance. She crossed the foyer and waited for a lift.

As the doors hissed open again on the sixth floor, Michelle could see the reception desk across the corridor. She stepped over and was greeted with a smile from the twenty-something brunette behind the desk.

"Good morning, can I help you?" the receptionist asked.

She gave her name then added "I'm starting here this morning. Mrs Farrell is expecting me," showing the receptionist her identity card.

"Oh, right, I'm Lucy Clarke. I'll tell Sylvia you're here."

Picking up the phone, Lucy tapped the extension number and waited for a reply.

"Ah, Sylvia, Michelle Hartley is here for you."

She put the phone down and turned to Michelle again and smiled. "Sylvia will be with you in a minute if you'd like to take a seat."

Thanking her, Michelle stepped over to the waiting area and sat down, taking care to do it in as demure a manner as she could manage, conscious of how she placed her legs and her overall posture.

After just a few minutes, a striking woman in a grey trouser suit approached her.

"Good morning, Michelle. Nice to meet you in person at last. That Zoom session was a bit of a pain, wasn't it?"

"It certainly was, but then difficulties are there to be overcome, aren't they?" Michelle responded, remembering a comment that Sylvia had made on the recording of the interview session.

"Yes, indeed. So how was your journey from Dubai? And have you settled into your apartment?"

"The journey was fine until the train crash."

"Oh my God, were you caught up in that? What a terrible atrocity. Were you hurt at all?"

"Not seriously. I'd been in the next carriage but I got up to use the loo shortly before the explosion. I was shaken around a bit and bent my nose but other than that, I was fine. Others in the compartment I'd been in weren't so lucky."

"How awful. Well, so long as you are OK. Would you like a coffee? Then we'll have a chat. I'll update you regarding the project then show you round the office and introduce you to a few key people. How does that sound?"

"It sounds fine and I'd love a coffee."

"OK – the kitchen is just here. There are a couple of filter machines. The rule is, if you empty a pot, you refill it – that way there's always a supply. Ignore that rule and you'll fall out with people when they find they have to wait for a fresh brew."

Having poured their coffees, they carried the mugs to Sylvia's office.

"Take a seat. Right, there have been some developments since we offered you the position. It's going to make the job significantly bigger."

"I see. Just how much bigger?"

"More than double the size."

Michelle put down her coffee and raised her eyebrows in query.

"Okay. And, I don't suppose we have twice as long to complete the work, do we?"

"Of course not," Sylvia replied with a smile. "As you know the original project was to replace the IT systems at Harding Distribution and bring them into the twenty-first century. It meant replacing all the computer equipment at their head office in Warrington and seventy sites across the north of England. They've now taken over two of their competitors which adds another hundred sites stretching from the Midlands into East Anglia and across Central Scotland."

Michelle looked up at the ceiling, visualising the additional complexities that the extra work would entail.

"Are they planning to consolidate all their back-office systems?"

"Yes, and before you ask, they're completely different systems – and incompatible," Sylvia told her.

Michelle shrugged her shoulders.

"Fine, if that's what they want then that's what we give them, I guess."

"Does the extra work worry you at all?

"No. It will take longer and cost more, obviously. The quicker they want it done, the more resources we'll have to put on it and the more expenditure that will incur. Merging the back-office systems isn't going to be cheap either. We'll need to carry out an audit and see what each of the current companies use, what they'll need in future and how we map the data from each existing system into the new one." Michelle replied.

Sylvia nodded her head.

"I'm glad to know you're comfortable with the increased work. There are a couple of other factors you need to take into consideration. The client is now building a new corporate headquarters which is projected to take fifteen months. That's the earliest you'll have access to the site for the new datacentre. And, of course, we can't roll out the desktop refresh until the servers are online."

"I see, I take it we'll be able to specify what services we need for the datacentre so that can be incorporated into the build?"

"Absolutely. In the meantime, we can be developing the applications and testing them. If the software development goes according to our initial estimates, there'll be a hiatus of a couple of months next autumn. It does mean if we hit problems with the applications, there'll be some leeway for us."

"That's good to know. I haven't yet done a project for a client where their requirements haven't been increased when they see what we can do. It'll make a change to know we've got a bit of spare time rather than having to try and squeeze the modifications into the original plan," Michelle replied.

"Yes, and within the original budget! One other thing, the office will be closed for two weeks over Christmas and New Year," Sylvia added.

"Fine, maybe I can get my nose fixed during the break."

"To be honest, until you mentioned it, I hadn't noticed anything but I imagine you're conscious of it. Right, let's go and introduce you to the key members of the team. You can leave your coat and bag in here."

The rest of the morning, Michelle spent being introduced to the members of the team including software and hardware engineers, Trainers, and support staff. She was reassured to see the team had the expertise to draw on that the project was going to demand over the next year or so.

After lunch, Sylvia asked her to come and meet the Managing Director. Lawrence Cavanagh was distinguished looking, a full head of short hair – his original dark brown now greying; about five foot ten tall and only a little surplus weight, he smiled in welcome as they were shown into his office by his secretary, Karen. He stood up and stepped around his striking oak desk, held out his hand to Michelle.

"Welcome to Cavanagh System Solutions, Michelle. I'm very glad to have you join us. Sylvia was most impressed with you during the interview."

He pointed to the corner seating area arranged in a U configuration.

"Sit down, please. Let me organise some coffee or would you prefer tea?"

"Coffee's fine, thank you."

Lawrence opened the door and leant round it.

"Karen, could you possibly make us some coffee? Thanks."

He turned back to Michelle and Sylvia, "Don't know what I'd do without Karen. Anyway, to business. Sylvia, have you told Michelle about the changes to the project?"

"Yes, I have," Sylvia confirmed. "Michelle wasn't at all fazed by the extra work."

"Good! Now, the client's commercial director, Robert Nicholls, he's Sir Robert, by the way, has been involved in projects in the past. They were all managed under PRINCE2. He knows what to expect using that modality and wants us to follow it. Does that pose a problem for you, Michelle?"

"No, not at all. We can set the project up using PRINCE2 and it'll work well for most of the hardware and training elements of the work. When it comes to software development, I imagine we'll use Agile methods so we end up with an integrated approach."

Lawrence smiled at Sylvia as they'd been discussing the same approach the previous week.

"Yes, that's what we had in mind," he confirmed. "Glad to know you're on the same track."

"How does the Commercial Director see himself as the Project Owner taking an overview or more closely involved as Senior User?" Michelle enquired.

"Definitely taking an overview as Project Owner," Lawrence stated.

"And has the client produced a formal Project Brief or a Project Initiation Document?" she asked – a smile appearing on her face. It would be a miracle if they had.

"Well, sort of. It's 'bring our IT systems up to date.' Obviously, our quotation makes a great many assumptions that form the basis of your brief."

"OK. Well, I suggest I take what we've got; produce a Project Brief and meet with Mr Nicholls to have it agreed and start to plan the detail."

"Excellent, Michelle. You made a first-rate choice here, Sylvia." Lawrence stood up and they followed suit.

Over the next two days, Michelle had meetings with the various workstream leaders and discussed the quotation that had been sent to the client and the likely time scales for their team's work. She sat down at her desk and prepared a draft Project Brief and outline plan. Having run this past Sylvia, she finalised the document and arranged a meeting with Robert Nicholls for the following Tuesday.

On Thursday afternoon, Michelle was making a coffee when Linda, the Training Manager, came into the kitchen.

"Hi, Michelle, in case no one else has mentioned it, some of us go out for a drink and meal on Friday evenings. You're welcome to join us. We meet in reception at five."

"Thanks, Linda, that sounds great. I think I'm going to need a chance to relax by then."

"I can imagine, you've really been dropped in at the deep end with this project, haven't you?"

"Yes, but that's what I expected; well, not quite, it's twice the size that they said during the interview – but that's par for the course with projects, isn't it?"

"I guess so. Well, you've made a good impression on most of the team and seem to know what you're doing."

"Only 'most' of the team?" Michelle queried.

"Ah, well, Bill Peterson is always awkward. He hates having women telling him what to do – so watch him carefully. If there's a chance to drop you in it, he will. He'll then casually mention it to Lawrence over a game of golf. They've worked together for twenty-odd years."

"Thanks for the heads up, Linda."

"Well, we girls have to stick together. Don't get me wrong, Bill knows his job; he's one of the best hardware engineers I know. He just thinks women should stick to female jobs. I'm fine because training is women's work. A couple of his engineers go along with his views as it's easier for them. Zoë's a big disappointment to him."

"What do you mean?"

"Sorry, I shouldn't have said that. Please ignore it," Linda pleaded.

Michelle didn't press the point. No doubt she'd find out soon enough – if it was important. If not, then it didn't matter. She finished pouring her drink.

"OK, I'll catch you later."

Chapter 14. The Weekend Starts Here

Friday morning, Michelle arrived at the entrance to the office block as Linda approached from the opposite direction, head down against the driving rain.

"OK for tonight?" Linda asked as they reached the door together and shook the rain off their umbrellas. She held the door open for Michelle to go through. Force of habit almost made Michelle insist that Linda went first but she managed to resist the inclination to be a gentleman. Once in the atrium, they walked over to the lifts.

"Definitely. I'm looking forward to it. Who will be there?"

Linda reeled off a list of names. "But not everyone will stop for the meal," she added.

"Quite a crowd then."

"Absolutely."

They separated as they entered their offices, Linda turned left at the reception desk, Michelle turned right.

The day was spent adding details to the draft project plan and creating a risk register for the project, helped by Max Ritter, a young German who provided administrative support for the project. He was a quiet lad with a good eye for detail.

"Aren't you coming with us for a drink this evening?" Michelle asked him.

"No, I have to attend college," he said.

"What are you studying?"

"Project Management. I want to be a Project Manager – like you, not just an admin assistant."

"Good for you. Let me know if you need any advice or have any questions. Maybe we can let you manage some aspects of the work. I'll mention it to Sylvia, if you like?"

"That would be very kind of you," he said in his stilted style.

"Fine. Well, I think we've done everything we can today – just log those notes and, when you've updated the files, you can leave."

Max dipped his head to one side.

"Thank you, Michelle."

He paused as though he wanted to say more.

"Was there something else?" Michelle asked.

"I just wanted to say that I am enjoying working with you. You have been patient with me and taken time to explain why we do things as we do."

Michelle realised that she probably wouldn't have done that when living as Jeff. Men tended to compete with each other; battling to be the alpha male. As Michelle, she found herself more inclined to work collaboratively, especially with the other women. Max, being so young, probably appeared more vulnerable than the older guys and didn't radiate the aggressiveness she'd been used to in male company.

She logged off her computer, picked up her bag and headed to the cloakroom to freshen up before meeting the others at reception.

As twenty would be too cumbersome for ordering drinks, the group split, mainly by teams; Michelle joining Linda's training set. She insisted on buying the first round for the five of them – settling on a bottle of Prosecco to celebrate the completion of her first week. They took their drinks to a long tall table where some of the others had already gathered. Several of the girls pulled up high bar stools to sit on while the guys stood around it.

Michelle scanned the group –testing herself to remember their names and their roles.

Bill dominated the end of the table so he could look down the entire three-metre length and see everyone – and ensure that they could see him. As usual at these events, Simon was standing next to him so they could chat about important matters – such as the chances of United ever winning the league again.

On the other side of Bill, Xavier, a southerner, provided a bridge to the training team. He was more interested in rugby than football; his heresy compounded by preferring Union to League. He was, nevertheless, male – even if he did do women's work as a trainer.

After finishing his first pint, Bill went outside for a smoke. It annoyed him that he could no longer enjoy his cigar inside the bar holding his glass in his other hand.

Seb, Sandra and Rosie got up at the same time and said goodnight.

Linda looked across the table at Simon, Zoë and Niamh.

"Are you three joining us for a meal?" she asked.

Niamh and Zoë looked at each other, then nodded at Linda.

"We're up for it," Niamh confirmed.

"I'm off," said Mel, draining her glass. "See you all on Monday."

"Me too," added Ash. "Have a good weekend."

"Shall we make a move then?" suggested Linda.

In the restaurant, Michelle sat at one end of the table with Zoë on one side and Linda on the other.

They took the menus the waiter handed them, then ordered drinks while deciding what to eat.

Michelle couldn't help noticing that Zoë's hands were rather larger than most of the women at the table and her shoulders somewhat broader. Her voice was also slightly husky. She knew there could be any number of reasons for these factors – but they could also point to a shared background.

Zoë slapped her menu down and turned to Michelle.

"Do you have a problem with me, Michelle? You've been giving me sideways glances ever since we sat down."

Michelle tried to give a surprised look.

"Of course I don't have a problem with you Zoë. Why would I?"

"Maybe you have something against transgender people? I'm sure you've realised that's what I am."

'If only you knew,' thought Michelle. But to say anything about her background would destroy her cover story.

"Are you? And why would that give me a problem?" she asked with furled eyebrows.

"Go on, tell me some of your best friends are trans!"

"No, I wouldn't go that far – but you aren't the first I've met." Well, that was certainly true.

"Really? Like where?"

"The Way Out Club in London? I went there a few times with a friend. That was before I started working in the Gulf. She introduced me to the girl who ran the club. I think her name was

Vicky," Michelle said. She didn't want to list all of the venues she'd been to; it could make Zoë wonder about her.

"OK. I believe you. Yes, Vicky Lee ran it. Probably still does. Sorry, but we get sensitive about people's reactions to us. All too often it's justified. We face a lot of discrimination – so often from TERFs making comments about protecting women's spaces. I wondered for a moment if you might be one."

"What's a TERF?" asked Linda, who'd been listening to the exchange.

Zoë looked at Michelle to see if she would answer; waiting to see if she knew what the acronym stood for.

Realising she was being challenged, Michelle replied.

"It stands for Trans Exclusionary Radical Feminist – a group of women who don't accept that transgender individuals should be considered women. And, no, I'm not one, Zoë. As far as I can see, transwomen aren't any threat." She was tempted to add '*as far as I'm concerned, you're as much of a woman as I am*' – but that might come back to bite her!

Zoë put her head to one side and looked at Michelle with a fresh expression that turned into a smile.

"Yeah? Well, if you're OK with trans people, maybe you'd like to go on afterwards to the Village? Of course, if you don't want to be seen out with a tranny, I understand."

Michelle hesitated. She'd only been to the Village a few times and her new hairstyle was very different to the 'Dolly Parton' wig she'd worn on past occasions – so the chances of being recognised were very slim. Maybe hiding in the open was a way of diverting attention.

"I told you, I used to have a trans friend so that doesn't worry me at all. Snag is, I'm not dressed for clubbing," she told her. "But, if you don't mind coming back to my apartment so I can get changed, you're on!"

"That suits me, do you mind if I get changed too? I've got my outfit in my bag." She pointed to a shoulder bag. "I usually change in the toilets here – then leave the bag in my car."

Chapter 15. The Village

The rain had finally cleared up leaving a clear sky. As they walked back to Michelle's apartment, Zoë turned to her.

"Manchester must be one hell of a change from Dubai."

"It certainly is. It would probably be about eighteen degrees this time of the evening; the high today would have been around thirty. No rain, of course."

"So, what brought you back to the UK and Manchester in particular?"

"I got tired of a misogynistic boss. So many of the guys out there seem to have the same alpha male ex-pat attitude. All that matters to them is money. It's all glitz and showing off." Michelle wasn't sure if this was true but was confident that Zoë wouldn't know any better.

"Says a woman with an Yves St Laurent handbag and wearing Jimmy Choo shoes – what did they cost? Couple of thousand between them?"

Michelle looked at Zoë, caught the twinkle in her eyes and recognised she was being teased. She shrugged her shoulders.

"Fair point. You couldn't afford to be left behind in the label stakes or you weren't taken seriously – no matter how good you were at your job."

Up in the flat, Zoë looked around and whistled.

"This is some place you've got."

"Thanks. Why don't you use the spare bedroom to change in? The bathroom's just there," Michelle said, pointing it out.

"Great, that's perfect."

As Zoë used the toilet, Michelle opened her wardrobe door and pulled out a couple of dresses. Hearing Zoë leave the bathroom, she went to her bedroom door.

"Which do you think, Zoë? The blue or the black?"

Zoë watched as Michelle held them in front of her in turn.

"You're going to make me look dowdy wearing either. But the blue looks fabulous."

It was thigh length, fitted at the top then flaring out from the waist with a bateau neckline edged in jewels. Much as she'd like to display some cleavage, she didn't have any to show off, so all the dresses she'd bought so far had high necklines.

"Blue it is then."

It was a little after ten o'clock when the taxi dropped them at the corner of Minshull Street and Canal Street. Michelle paid the driver then joined Zoë on the pavement.

"We'll walk down Canal Street, have you been here before?" Zoë asked.

Sticking to her cover story, Michelle said she hadn't. In fact, she'd been at this very spot just before the Covid lockdown started nineteen months earlier and had eaten in the restaurant they were now walking past. Before that, she had visited the Gay Village a handful of times over the years.

"So, where are we going?" she asked.

"Churchill's. It's down on the next corner."

Michelle remembered Churchill's from her last visit.

"Fine. You're the guide."

Zoë nodded to the doorperson as they went in the side entrance. They were immediately assaulted by the beat of the dance music and had to struggle through the crowd to get to the bar.

"What are you having, Michelle?" Zoë shouted.

"Chardonnay please," she replied.

It took a few minutes to attract the attention of the bar staff but they were finally served their drinks.

"Cheers," Michelle said, tapping her glass against Zoë's

"Cheers," Zoë replied. "Look, I'm sorry about earlier – accusing you of having an issue with me because I'm trans."

"I understand and I'm sorry if I made you feel uncomfortable. I admit that I wondered if you might be – but only because I was aware of some of the signs."

"How was that? Was it because your friend was trans?"

"Yes, I met a few others at the time. Some were obvious, big hands, prominent Adam's Apple, deep voices, five o'clock shadow; well, you know the things I mean."

"Don't I just! Doesn't help when you've been known as one gender then start living as another. Bill Peterson really can't get his head round it. He thinks I'm mad. As far as he's concerned, men are the dominant sex and it's inconceivable that anyone would want to change to the lesser sex."

"Well, that's his problem," Michelle said. "Are we going to dance?"

"Absolutely."

They drained their glasses – leaving them to be spiked wasn't an option – then joined the crowd on the dance floor.

Zoë weaved between other dancers to join a group of her friends, followed by Michelle. Zoë shouted introductions – but the names were lost in the booming bass rhythm from huge speakers. Eventually, they took a break and, in the queue for the ladies' loos, she was able to introduce Michelle to the others.

By the time Michelle got home, having taken a taxi from the village, it was well past midnight. Zoë had gone on to another club with her friends.

After undressing and cleansing and toning her face, she slid between the sheets. She felt torn about hiding her background from Zoë – but there really wasn't any option.

Michelle slept late on Saturday morning – there were no immediate matters requiring her attention. As she woke, driving rain was rattling against the windows. Pulling the duvet up under her chin and laying back on the pillow, she reviewed her situation.

She'd clearly been accepted at the office. Nobody doubted that she was the Michelle who'd been appointed to the role – why would they? Going out 'dressed' previously, there was always the risk of 'being made' due to a slip-up in her behaviour drawing attention. But Michelle's back story precluded any possible questions along those lines. In any case, presenting as Michelle just felt completely natural – especially since the hair-do and beauty treatments. Wigs were always one of the easiest ways to spot a cross-dresser.

The project was a challenge – but nothing that couldn't be managed; the next steps in planning it would depend on the outcome of the meeting with Robert Nicholls on Tuesday. The flat was sorted and her appointment with the gender specialist was booked for Wednesday evening. She could do some more clothes shopping, of course; which reminded her that she did need to go to the supermarket – although even that could wait until tomorrow.

The several glasses of Prosecco and Chardonnay she'd drunk last night started to make their presence felt so, throwing back the bedclothes, Michelle swung her legs onto the floor and headed for the bathroom. Ablutions completed, she wandered into the kitchen, made a coffee, toasted some bread and took her breakfast into the lounge.

No doubt Charlotte and Jessica would be at the riding stables. *'Were they missing her?'* she wondered, feeling pangs of guilt about any hurt she was causing them. She missed them and wished there'd been another way of dealing with his issues. But, there hadn't been any alternative, had there? Living as Jeff had become a lie; it wasn't who she was. Hiding her true nature had impacted on her relationship with Deborah and, if she was honest, contributed to Deb's infidelity. Or had it? Michelle suspected that Deborah had started having affairs a long time before Jeff decided he needed to transition. On the other hand, maybe it had been his gender issues that had affected his sex drive even before it surfaced completely. Maybe his perfunctory performances had driven Deborah into other men's beds.

Not that it mattered any longer. Michelle was committed to her new life and determined to make a success of it; wherever it led.

She popped the last piece of toast, dripping in butter and lime marmalade into her mouth and drained the last of the coffee. Having put the mug and plate into the dishwasher, she wiped down the kitchen surface then dressed. In view of the weather, she decided on denim jeans and a thick brown cable knit jumper and tan ankle boots with a two-inch heel.

Taking the lift down to the garage level, she unlocked her car and drove to the supermarket.

Chapter 16. Tuesday: The Client's Lair

Michelle met Sylvia at the office before they drove over to Harding Distribution for the appointment with Robert Nicholls. The client's premises were on the outskirts of Warrington, a half-hour drive from their office.

Drawing up outside a typical commercial unit on one of the industrial estates, Michelle parked in a visitors' space and followed Sylvia into the building through glass doors on the corner.

Having given their names to the blonde receptionist, they sat down on orange modular chairs. Michelle glanced around. The walls were a nondescript beige. The company's name in Futura font together with product photographs in black-edged frames were displayed around the walls. The look was definitely 1990s she decided.

'Was that a reflection of the company as a whole?' She wondered.

A few minutes later, there was the click, click of high heels descending the wooden stairs leading to the first floor. A smartly dressed woman of indeterminate age approached them.

"Mrs Farrell? Miss Hartley? Would you come this way please?"

Sylvia and Michelle followed her up the stairs, past more product photographs in black frames. At the top, they turned onto a corridor with light oak doors leading to offices off each side. The walls matched those in reception while a dark orange carpet had, presumably, been laid to reflect the modular seating downstairs – or had the modular seating been bought to match the carpets? Someone must have thought this was quite Avant Garde thirty years ago.

Their guide opened a door bearing a sign that announced that it was the boardroom and gestured for them to enter.

"Mr Nicholls will join you in a moment, please help yourself to coffee or tea," she said, pointing to a side table bearing cups and saucers and silver vacuum flasks.

Sylvia poured cups and added milk for each of them while Michelle took out the papers she'd prepared for the meeting. As they finished their tasks, the door opened to admit a tall male with well-trimmed greying hair and matching beard and moustache; his ruddy, weather-beaten, complexion suggested a great percentage of his time spent outside – rather than behind a desk. His age could have been anything from early forties to late fifties.

"Good morning, Sylvia," the newcomer announced as he stepped towards Michelle, extending his hand. "I assume you're Michelle, I'm Craig Mann, Robert Nicholls is just finishing a phone call, he'll be with us shortly."

Michelle realised that this was the client's Project Manager as she shook his hand.

"Yes, pleased to meet you, Craig, can I get you a coffee?"

"It should be me offering you as we're the hosts; but yes, thank you. White with two sugars, please."

Just as she was handing Craig his coffee, the door opened again to admit the client's Commercial Director followed by the woman who had shown them up from reception.

"Good morning, Sylvia. Sorry to keep you waiting," he announced as they shook hands. He turned to Michelle. "I'm Robert Nicholls – as I'm sure you've worked out. Glad to meet you, my dear."

"Coffee, Sir Robert?" asked the woman.

"Yes, thank you, Audrey," he replied. "She's the only one who uses my title. It's stuff and nonsense of course. Right, shall we get on with the meeting? Audrey will take minutes for us."

They took their places at the table. Michelle had placed a folder containing various documents at each seat together with a separate sheet with an agenda.

"Thank you, Sir Robert." Stuff and nonsense *he* might call it, but it wouldn't do any harm to be respectful. "I'm aware that you have used PRINCE2 to manage projects in the past and have asked that we use the same modality. I have, therefore, prepared a draft Project Brief outlining the objectives, time frame, scope, constraints including budgets, quality considerations, risks etc. for discussion. I've also drafted an outline Project Plan to indicate our approach."

They turned to the first of the documents and went through it point by point making any changes that were required.

"That was a very comprehensive brief, Sylvia," Sir Robert said as they agreed the final point. "I'm confident that we made the right choice appointing Cavanagh Systems. I'm impressed. What do you think Craig?"

Craig gave a somewhat lukewarm acknowledgement.

"Michelle did most of the work on the Brief and on the Plan which we'll look at next," Sylvia pointed out, smiling at her.

"Shall we take a fifteen-minute comfort break at this point?" suggested Nicholls. "I could certainly do with it."

While Robert Nicholls left the room for a few minutes, Audrey disappeared to organise some fresh coffee. Michelle, Sylvia and Craig remained in the boardroom. He coughed then turned to them.

"Of course, drafting plans is one thing, Michelle. But do you have any problems getting men to take you seriously? Part of this project will involve construction and, in my experience, it's a very masculine environment. It takes a particular kind of woman to impose her will on engineers working in that field."

Michelle and Sylvia exchanged glances but were saved from responding by Audrey returning with fresh flasks of coffee, followed by Nicholls.

They resumed their seats and took up the draft project plan.

"I've assumed that you, Sir Robert, will be the Project Owner and chair the Project Board and that Mr Mann will be the Senior User and handle day-to-day liaison on behalf of Harding's. Sylvia will be the Senior Supplier and I will be the Project Manager. We've also appointed Malcolm Ellis as Project Assurance to ensure that our processes are appropriate.

She then explained how the project would be split into various workstreams each, effectively, managed as a sub-project.

"The first priority will be to undertake an audit of your existing systems and those of the companies you've recently acquired; determine what you need from all parts of the proposed system and how it will be used. Once we understand what you need to do and how, we can start to design and test the individual modules," Michelle explained. "During the audit, we'll also identify what data is held in the three current systems and how that will need to be mapped to the new database fields."

"That sounds sensible," Sir Robert agreed. Once more, Craig Mann grudgingly indicated his agreement with his boss.

"I anticipate the audit phase taking us through to Christmas. During quarter one of 2022, we can create the new database structure and carry out some test migrations of existing data. We will also start to design the different modules for the system."

"You realise the building for the new servers won't be ready until the beginning of 2023? How will you test the systems?" asked Craig – smugly thinking he'd identified a flaw in the women's work.

"That's not a problem. Testing will involve far fewer transactions than the live system – our development datacentre is adequate for that purpose," Michelle responded with a smile.

Mann's brow furrowed as he looked down at the papers in front of him.

They continued to work through the outline plan touching lightly on desktop equipment, network requirements, training on the updated general office systems as well as the specialist applications and finishing with plans for communicating the changes to staff and customers.

"You're going to have to watch Craig Mann, Michelle," Sylvia remarked as they drove out of the car park.

Chapter 17. Wednesday: Consultation

Michelle was apprehensive as she clicked on the Zoom link for her appointment with the online gender specialist. She needed to provide a credible background story if she was to get the treatment she wanted.

As Jeff, she could have explained how she'd gradually realised that presenting as a man involved playing a role that no longer fitted how she identified. That still applied – but she had to adjust the context. `

She watched as the Zoom screen loaded – displaying a message to say the session organiser would admit her shortly. She'd hardly had time to read it when the screen changed to show her image on the left and the specialist on the right.

"Good evening, Michelle, how are you? I'm Fiona, I'll be taking you through this initial session."

The image looking back at Michelle was of a woman about her own age, perhaps a year or two older, with shoulder-length auburn hair framing a welcoming face. The caption gave her name and pronouns 'she/her'

"Hi Fiona, good to meet you. I'm fine thanks, how about you?"

"Yes, fine too. So let me run through a few ground rules for the session. As I said, my name is Fiona and I'm one of the counsellors here. Let me say, immediately, that there is no 'pass' or 'fail' for this consultation. Our aim is to identify the right steps for you and to see how we can best help you achieve your objectives. Are you OK with that?"

Michelle wasn't 100 per cent convinced by Fiona's assurance that her story wouldn't be judged – there must be occasions when someone approached them for treatment that wouldn't be appropriate. In her case, however, she was sure that a full transition, including surgery, was the right course. So, she concurred with Fiona's remarks.

"As far as my background is concerned, I've been working with transgender clients for seven years. I'm fully qualified as a counsellor and accredited by the relevant professional body. I've probably worked with more than four hundred gender-variant individuals. How does that sound?"

"It sounds like you should know what you're doing," Michelle responded.

"I certainly hope so. Now, everything you tell us is confidential and will not be revealed outside our organisation without your permission – with a few important exceptions. These are: first if we are compelled to provide information by a court of law. That's generally only in cases of terrorism or money laundering. Secondly, where we are obliged to report incidents under child protection legislation; thirdly where there is a risk of or actual serious harm by the client to themselves or others. Are you happy with those limitations?"

"Absolutely," replied Michelle – thinking that she'd better keep quiet about the money she'd found when taking over Michelle's identity.

"I also need to cover the 'Disclosure of Protected Information' under the Gender Recognition Act. Are you aware of the restrictions?"

"I'm not sure," Michelle replied.

"Basically, with some exceptions, it's illegal to reveal that someone has applied for a Gender Recognition Certificate – or, if someone has a GRC, to reveal their history. This could prevent the organisation from referring you to other services including surgery unless you give permission. We ask, therefore that you give us permission to disclose 'protected information' where necessary to obtain support or services you require. Is that OK with you?"

"Yes, of course."

"Fine. So, now those formalities are out of the way, why don't you tell me about yourself, why you've contacted us and what you want to achieve?"

Michelle saw that Fiona had sat back in her chair slightly though she had a pad by her right hand ready to take notes.

"I've worn female clothes whenever I had the chance almost as long as I can remember, certainly from my early teens, if not earlier. Until about a year ago, I'd have described it as cross-dressing but over the last couple of years, I've found that dressing and presenting as a male felt more and more like a role I was playing rather than the other way round. I've now started working full-time as Michelle."

"Does your employer know of your history?"

This was one of the questions that Michelle had been concerned about. She could hardly tell Fiona the truth – but would the gender team dig deeper into her background and find the discrepancies? How would she have managed the interview process if her employers hadn't known her background? She had decided that, if asked, she'd have to pretend that they were aware of her transition.

"My immediate manager, the Head of HR and the Managing Director know – but no one else in the company is aware of my background and that's how I'd like it to remain."

"And, there's no reason why they should know unless you decide to tell them. We certainly wouldn't inform them. How did you get the job though?"

"I'd been working overseas for several years but wanted to return to the UK to transition and the position came up. As no one was meeting face to face at the time, there was no problem with me being interviewed over Zoom and I was able to lease an apartment the same way."

"You say you want to transition fully. What do you mean by that?"

"I want to undergo medical treatment including hormones and lower surgery to make my body as female as possible; perhaps even breast augmentation and facial feminisation. Fortunately, I don't have a prominent Adams Apple and I think my voice is reasonably feminine – I've always had a talent for mimicry and that helps."

"I'd certainly agree about your voice. It's fine and your facial features are already feminine. As you probably realise, breast development on hormones will take time and you won't see the full benefit for a year or two after surgery. Can I ask if you have the resources to fund the treatment you are planning or will you need any of it on the NHS?"

"Funding won't be a problem. I was well paid working overseas. I hear what you're saying about the facial feminisation – but I just feel that my chin could be a bit softer and I'd like to do something about my cheekbones."

Michelle could hardly explain that the real reason for the facial surgery was to match the original Michelle's passport photograph.

"Well, that's entirely up to you. How soon did you propose commencing treatment?"

"As soon as possible for the hormones – yesterday would be ideal." Michelle joked.

"Well, it might take a few weeks. We need you to have blood tests first."

"I've already arranged those. You'll have them by the end of the week."

"Fine. We seem to have jumped ahead of ourselves a little here. Let's go through the assessment form you completed online."

Over the next hour and a half, Fiona discussed Michelle's responses to the questionnaire that had covered her earliest memories in respect of her gender identity (at least as early as eleven or twelve). Her family background (no siblings and both parents dead; not in touch with any extended family). Whether she had professional support in place including counselling? (No, she needed to register with an NHS doctor locally). Was she active in any LGBT or trans support groups? (No, and she preferred to remain stealth).

At the end of the session, Fiona said she was happy to refer Michelle to the team's medical staff for treatment and she saw no reason why she shouldn't be prescribed hormones in the near future.

"One of the team will be in touch over the next few days to arrange a medical consultation. If you have no other questions, I'll say good night and good luck."

After thanking Fiona, Michelle closed down her laptop. Sat back in her chair and took a few deep breaths then stood up and poured herself a very large white wine.

Chapter 18. Jeff's Funeral

Michelle logged onto her tablet planning to read for a few minutes before preparing dinner when she saw a notification about the funeral of one of the train bombing victims. She was startled to realise that it was 'Jeff's' funeral that was being covered. She clicked through to the Surrey newspaper website.

A shiver went down her spine as she read that the victim's widow, Deborah Shaw, was accompanied by her two children, Charlotte and Jessica and her parents, Mr & Mrs Donaldson. A lump formed in her throat as she stared at the photo of the two girls holding their grandparents' hands. She wondered, again, if there had been any other way she could have handled the dilemma she'd faced over transition.

There seemed to be several onlookers in the photographs outside the crematorium – probably curiosity seekers and other newspaper reporters – but not many faces that she recognised; with one exception. Standing at Deborah's shoulder was Oliver Matthews. He gave the air of proprietorship – not just that of a family friend being supportive.

It was confirmation of what Michelle had suspected.

Further down the web page, a video piece showed Deborah's father, Edward Donaldson, eulogising his son-in-law; praising him as a family man who'd been tragically caught up in the terrorist atrocity. He praised how Jeffrey had provided for his family and how they always came first for him. Edward also urged the authorities to take action against the Islamists who appeared to be responsible for the atrocity. Deborah nodded her head, wiping the corner of her eye with a handkerchief and the girls clung to their grandmother as he spoke about how Jeffrey would be missed.

Knowing Deborah, the scene felt staged to Michelle. Or, perhaps, she didn't want the family's grief to be genuine. It was a quandary. She wanted her daughters to get over the loss of their father – but she also wanted them to miss him; at least a little.

Michelle realised the cremation did mean there was now, no possibility of the substitution being discovered. She wondered what Deborah would do with the ashes. Would she follow the request in Jeff's will that they be scattered at sea? He'd added the request when making his will and his solicitor and sailing partner had asked how he wanted his remains to be dealt with. It had been a spur-of-the-moment decision but, as Glen had spent most of his life at sea, it did seem appropriate for his ashes to end up on the waves.

She left the tablet on the table and poured a large glass of wine then drank a toast to Jeff, Glen and the original Michelle. She wondered if Michelle's body had been given a decent send-off too – or was it still being held in a mortuary somewhere? Would it be buried or cremated as 'Yvette Williamson', the name on the ID she'd left on the train? Or would the police have established that as fake?

Chapter 19. Fanning the Flames

P eter Holmes, leader of Action 4 England, turned to his deputy, Tommy James, as they looked at the same web article.

"Excellent, just what we needed. Let's take advantage of public anger; get the troops out collecting for families of those affected by terrorist outrages who need support. Not that that family is short of a bob or two in any case. The grandfather seemed sympathetic to our aims – see if we can use them on posters."

"Maybe he'd be prepared to speak at meetings, too, Peter."

"Good idea – sound him out."

Chapter 20. Popping Pills

J ust as Fiona had suggested it would, Michelle's medical consultation went smoothly and the gender specialist was happy to prescribe HRT for her. The blood tests had been fine and the clinic had checked her blood pressure and cholesterol levels at the same time as taking their samples. Not that Michelle had had any reason to expect any other result. Her work might involve sitting at her computer or in meetings much of the time but she watched her diet and had always exercised.

As Jeff, she'd tried to fit in at least four sessions at the gym every week – spending time on treadmills, bikes, rowing machines and other apparatus before thirty lengths of the swimming pool. Jeff's gym membership had entitled him to use clubs around the country – so, even when he was away on business, there was usually a venue he could access. As Michelle, swimming had been curtailed as most gyms and leisure centres had limited individual cubicles and she could hardly use communal changing facilities. Fortunately, she was still able to exercise in the gym in the apartment block – changing and showering in her own flat.

The promised prescription arrived a few days later; Michelle wasted no time filling the script at a local chemist. Before handing over the prescription, the pharmacist asked Michelle if she could have a quick chat about the medication.

"Have you had these before?" she asked.

Michelle confirmed that she hadn't.

"Have the risks involved been explained to you?"

"Yes, the specialist said there is an increased risk of breast cancer and heart disease."

"And you're happy to accept those risks?"

"Under the circumstances, there isn't much alternative."

The pharmacist looked at her.

"You realise you can get the prescription on the NHS rather than paying privately, don't you?"

"Yes, but I've only recently moved to the area and haven't registered with a GP yet."

"Well, if you're looking for one with experience of transgender patients, I can suggest two or three options."

Taken aback by the suggestion, she asked "Why would you think that would be relevant to me?"

"Certainly not because of anything you've said or your appearance or anything like that. I recognise the name of the clinic that issued the prescription and know what they do. Several of their patients are customers."

"I see," she said trying to recover her composure.

"You seem concerned, don't be. I was just trying to be helpful. My colleagues and I are totally professional and your medical needs are entirely your business."

Outside, Michelle slid behind the wheel of her car and just sat there for a while. She'd been shaken by the pharmacist's observation. The plan had been to have complete separation between Michelle and Jeff or Glen – and to be able to adopt Michelle's identity as though she had always been her. That hadn't worked out quite as cleanly as she'd hoped. The gender clinic had needed to know that she was transitioning – or she wouldn't have been able to get a referral later for surgery. Perhaps it was just bad luck that the pharmacist recognised the clinic's name and knew what services they provided.

The question was, did this pose any further risks for her?

Was there any reason for either the clinic or the pharmacy to delve deeper into Michelle's history? What about when she registered with a GP? They would definitely need to know that she was transgender.

The important consideration was to avoid any connection with Jeff.

Using Glen as background would work. He'd been born in the UK so had a local birth certificate – even if he had been an Australian citizen and passport holder. He might even have had an NHS number which could be traced to register with a GP. It wasn't likely that the GP would want to know where she worked – but if they did, she could use the explanation she'd given the gender clinic, that the MD, her line manager and the head of HR knew her history but she wanted it kept confidential.

The one significant hole in her story was that Glen had been a sailor – so how would he have qualified as a project manager? Walter Scott's quotation about weaving tangled webs came to mind.

Well, she decided, there wasn't much she could do about it now. She was far too committed to her new life for any U-turns at this stage. She'd just have to be ultra-careful to keep her story straight.

With that, Michelle turned the ignition key and the engine burst into life. She reversed out of the parking place and drove back to the Quays. Back in her apartment, she had a little ceremony to take her first small round pill – wondering how long it would be before she noticed any changes.

Chapter 21. Christmas

Michelle had told Sylvia that she would take advantage of the Christmas break to have her nose reconstructed after injuring it in the train crash. Whilst she did, indeed, plan to have some work done on it, she was more interested in softening her chin line, having her brow shaved slightly and heightening her cheekbones. Her features weren't that dissimilar to the photograph in Michelle's passport but the changes would reduce even those slight variations – and, with the feminising effects of the HRT, add to the difference between her old appearance as Jeff and her new appearance as Michelle.

As Christmas approached, the project was on track and there was no problem booking two weeks leave for the surgery. Adding bank holidays, she had nearly three weeks before returning to work. With luck, most of the swelling would have subsided by that time and any residual bruising could be concealed with make-up.

The surgeon was pleased with the results and Michelle was able to leave the hospital, after two nights, on Christmas Eve. It was only a short taxi drive to her apartment.

She hadn't bothered to decorate the flat for the holidays – there hadn't been any point; Christmas was for children after all.

All she had were a few Christmas and get-well cards from her colleagues on the bookcase. She didn't dislike Christmas; in fact, she quite enjoyed the traditional music and general festivities though not the greedy commercialisation. Back home, she would have happily stood, with the family, outside her door to listen to the carol singers making their way along the street. There had been nothing like that around the quays and only the Pogues, Slade, Chris Rhea and their ilk trying to get the supermarket shoppers into a festive spirit.

Although the flat was unadorned, the fridge and freezer were well stocked for the holiday – a precaution she'd taken before going into hospital to avoid the last-minute panic buying. There was a turkey dinner for one, an individual Christmas pudding and a small tub of brandy butter for tomorrow. They would have to wait as she was restricted to liquids only for a couple of days – then soft foods to give her jaw a chance to recover. This evening, she'd settle for a bowl of soup in front of the television.

Michelle's first thoughts when she woke on Christmas day were of the family she'd abandoned.

Would Charlotte, Jessica and Deborah be at home in Surrey or spending the holiday with Deborah's parents in Tonbridge? Or had they gone ahead with the skiing trip to Chamonix that Jeff had booked earlier in the year?

Would the girls still be excited enough to have woken early and been eager to open their presents? Or had they been content to wait until their mother had stirred? Would they have settled for the stockings with silly bits and pieces that family tradition called to be left on the end of their beds?

What would Deborah have bought them for their main gifts? No doubt it would be something to do with riding.

Would the children give any thought for their father?

A lump formed in her throat and a tear slipped down her cheek as Michelle contemplated the situation.

Would Oliver Matthews be with Deborah? Probably not if they were at her parents – but almost certainly if they were at home or in Chamonix. If he was, Michelle could hardly complain – but she still felt a tinge of jealousy. Not so much for taking Deborah's affection but for potentially taking his place as the children's father. It didn't matter that she had abrogated any right to that role. It still had the power to hurt.

Becoming Michelle had been Jeff's dream – and it was still what she needed to do if she was to survive –let alone live a fulfilling life. But the price had been high.

She was now on her own. Making friends was fraught with danger – especially at this stage. She couldn't be open about her history and, if you have to hide your true self from people, building relationships was difficult. She certainly couldn't even consider romantic liaisons until she'd undergone surgery. Whether she'd find anyone after that remained to be seen; she'd heard of a few trans women and men finding long-term partners – but that did seem to be the minority.

So, was she destined to be on her own? Perhaps; but given a choice of living a lie in a meaningless relationship or being her real self but alone she knew she'd made the right decision for her.

In any case, it was too late to go back now. She was committed to being Michelle.

With that thought, she threw back the duvet, swung her legs out of the bed and stood up; feeling the hem of her silk nightdress fall down around her legs; a sensation that she still loved – so much nicer than cotton pyjama trousers.

She went into the kitchen and made a mug of coffee which she took into the lounge. The day stretched out ahead of her. She didn't have any plans and no one would be coming to call. Standing by the window she looked out over the quays. The skies were clear – and the forecast was for it to cloud over but remain dry. Perhaps she'd go for a walk. Someone at the office had mentioned Rivington Reservoirs as a great place for a hike.

After breakfast, she showered then dressed in warm clothes.

The roads out to Rivington were virtually deserted – even on the motorways there was just a handful of other vehicles. As she got out of her car to change her shoes for boots, the wind cut into her until she'd pulled on her walking jacket.

According to the application on her phone, circumnavigating the lower reservoir was four and a half miles – she 'walked' that distance, and more, regularly on the treadmills at the gym so it wasn't much of a physical challenge.

Stamping her feet to settle them in her boots, she slipped a soft snood over her head to protect the tape covering her surgeries, then pulled up the tall jacket collar and hood. With the drawstring tightened, only her eyes were exposed to the elements. Happy she was well prepared; she strode out of the car park.

The trees were, for the most part, bare of any foliage and there was little wildlife visible – just the occasional squirrel and a few birds squawking overhead.

The tops of the surrounding hills were still snow-covered from falls earlier in the month – no doubt adding to the sharpness of the wind. A wind that relentlessly drove clouds across the sky – their shadows scudding over the surface of the reservoir broken into white horses by those same gusts. The air smelled fresher than around the quays – but lacked the scents that would be present later in the year from foliage and blossoms and the higher moorland's gorse and heather. All that remained was the smell of damp decaying leaves.

Settling into a steady pace, Michelle tried to concentrate on her surroundings – but, inevitably, her thoughts returned to the children. Would they also be out for a walk? If she'd been with them, they certainly would be out – but Deborah wasn't keen on the outdoors – unless on a horse. Perhaps they'd be out for a ride? Or, maybe they'd be at the stables, schooling their ponies?

Feeling the sharp wind making her eyes water, she wiped the tear away and blew her nose.

Ninety minutes later she was back at the car. Her skin was glowing with the exertion – though she was glad to get out of the wind and let the heater warm her.

Chapter 22. Letter from Liechtenstein

On Wednesday, after picking up some milk from the nearby mini supermarket, Michelle collected her mail.

There were a few circulars in flimsy manila and white window envelopes and a weightier white envelope with the addressee hand-written, bearing a Liechtenstein stamp. Back in the flat, she put the circulars to one side while she opened the hand-written envelope. It contained two pages from a private commercial bank in the principality. She nearly choked on her drink as she read that the writer had pleasure to confirm receipt of one million seven hundred and sixty-five thousand Euros.

She read the paragraph again – half expecting it to say something different – but it remained the same.

The letter went on to state that the bank had invested the sum, as instructed, in government bonds. Attached was a handwritten statement giving details of the investments.

It was like winning the lottery – but it raised questions. The cash she'd found in an envelope in Michelle's handbag and the current account bank balance could be accounted for by higher salaries and limited expenses in Dubai; but there was no way Michelle could have earned one and a half a million pounds. So where had it come from? While chatting on the train, she'd mentioned her parents had died in a car accident a few months ago – so, maybe insurance or from the sale of a house? But why use a private bank in Liechtenstein? It was like something out of James Bond!

She stared at the letter – as if it would reveal the story behind the money.

If it had been gained illegally, it could threaten her future. IF? The reality was that unless it was from her parents, that was the only likely answer.

The first step was to check probate records. If that showed that Michelle had inherited the money, all would be fine. If not, she wasn't sure what she'd do.

Had she known about this before committing herself to living in role, maybe she'd have walked away from the opportunity. She certainly didn't like the idea of having to look over her shoulder all the time in case someone had traced her and wanted their money back.

She fetched the file of Michelle's documents. It contained 'her' birth certificate. Michelle Samantha Hartley, born 24th November 1985. Her parents were listed as father: Norman Keith Hartley; mother Muriel Joan Hartley formerly Fraser.

Hoping that the Hartleys hadn't divorced and remarried, she entered the names on the dot Gov dot UK website. The search produced records of Norman Keith and Muriel Joan Hartley with 29th November 2020 as the date of death for both of them. It looked as though she'd found the right records. Hopefully, the probate record would show how much the estate had been worth and the will would indicate if it had been left to Michelle.

To get further details, she'd had to register with the site and pay a fee of £1.50 for each record.

Michelle paused for a moment. Would registering and paying for the searches raise any alarms? It didn't seem likely. The request would, apparently, be from their daughter and nothing would be more natural, surely? Besides which, why would anyone investigate requests for records – they wouldn't have the time, would they?

Satisfied that the risk of complications was minimal, she entered her credit card details into the system and waited for the display to indicate that she could download the records. When it didn't change from 'pending', she searched the help file and found that the records wouldn't necessarily be available immediately – but they'd email her when they were ready to download.

Frustrated by the delay, she closed the laptop. She would just have to be patient.

The following day, Michelle checked her emails and saw there was one from Probate Search showing her order was complete. She clicked the link and downloaded the files. The Grant of Probate showed that the total value of the estate was just over £170,000 – enough to account for much of the balance in her UK accounts but not the deposit in Liechtenstein.

'*Shit!*' she thought. This was a complication she hadn't considered when she'd seen the two dead bodies lying in the carriage and decided to switch identities.

The question was, where had the money come from? The most likely answer was from her previous employment in the Gulf.

How did she get it? That was another question.

Perhaps it was from rounding up or down charges on transactions and siphoning off tiny fractions of a per cent. Michelle had been responsible for commissioning the IT system, she also had experience of coding, so it would have been possible for her to make changes to the software.

Was that what she'd done?

How likely was it that the embezzlement would be discovered?

Michelle was obviously very clever and would have planned to get away with the theft. So, maybe it hadn't been discovered. Or, if it had been, perhaps the bank was avoiding publicity by keeping quiet about the loss. Even so, they could still be looking for her behind the scenes.

Finding her wineglass was empty, she walked into the kitchen, took the open bottle from the fridge and refilled her glass. There was only a little left in the bottle so she took a couple of mouthfuls – then topped it up. As she dropped the empty bottle in her recycling bin, she wondered if she was drinking too much. The thought didn't last long, however, as she took another bottle from her store and put it in the fridge to chill.

Taking her glass with her, she returned to the lounge and considered her situation again.

It had been nearly three months since Michelle had returned to the UK. If her previous employers *had* discovered the loss, surely that would have been sufficient time for them to have traced her.

What were her options?

Could she return the funds – before the loss was discovered?

Would that help?

Had Michelle kept a note of how she'd embezzled the funds – *if* that's what she'd done?

If she had, was it likely to be on her laptop? On a secure memory stick? Or a memory card? It might even have been loaded into an account in the cloud. Trying to find it would be like looking for a needle, that might not even exist, in several haystacks.

To complicate any search, the file, if it existed, wouldn't be easily recognisable – it wasn't likely to be as simple as a document file, even if it was password-protected or hidden.

So, how had her predecessor done it? How would *she* do it?

She doubted if it was in a hidden document – it would be relatively easy to list all hidden files and reset the attributes. And that would massively reduce the number of files that would need to be examined.

Had she just renamed the document file to, say, .JPG or MP3 and stored it amongst other photographs or music files? Was it an executable file? Or some other common file type that bloated storage requirements on modern computers?

Michelle powered up the laptop and discovered it held more than 65,000 files. How long would it take to scan through so many files? A quick experiment suggested 1 second for a simple file but longer if she needed to scroll through longer or multi-page documents. Even two seconds per file would take more than thirty-six hours. And that was just files on the laptop.

If the file was in the cloud, she'd probably never find it.

Michelle still had ten days before she was due back in the office, probably sufficient time to check the laptop, then decide what to do.

Chapter 23. Hurry Up and Wait

The search of the laptop had been in vain. Michelle found nothing to explain the one and a half million pounds – despite nearly seventy hours checking files until her eyes blurred and her bottom was numb from so long in the chair; not to mention jug after jug of strong coffee increasing her adrenalin – and her nervousness.

She carefully considered her options.

Not knowing how the money had been acquired meant it was impossible to simply return it and hope that no one would ever know it had gone missing.

She could admit what she'd done – but to whom? The police? Michelle's previous employers?

If she admitted to the police that she'd adopted Michelle's (and Glen's) identities, she'd certainly face charges of identity theft – and stealing their funds. Those both carried custodial sentences – and where would she be imprisoned? A male establishment or a female one? She didn't have a Gender Recognition Certificate so was still legally male – and any physical search would show she was physically male. The possibility of being held in a male prison was frightening.

Would Michelle's previous employers be more helpful? Perhaps, if that's where the money had come from. Perhaps they'd be happy to recover their loss and avoid adverse publicity. But what if it hadn't come from there? What if it had been acquired elsewhere – maybe from other criminal sources? Where would that leave her?

Either option also involved exposing her past and that Jeff hadn't died in the train crash. The insurance company would demand their money back and the family would be destitute. The children would never forgive their father for the deception let alone losing their comfortable lifestyle. That had to be avoided if at all possible.

After evaluating the alternatives, the risks and consequences, Michelle decided to remain as she was and hope, and pray, her predecessor had been clever enough to avoid discovery. Time alone would tell if this was the right decision.

Once she was back at work, she threw herself into the project.

Before Christmas, the team had carried out an extensive audit of the systems used by the client's three different divisions; they'd held workshops with all of the departments that would be using the system to identify perceived shortcomings with the old applications and features the staff would like incorporated in the design and arrived at a specification that had been approved by the project board.

Now it was down to the system architects and programmers to produce the various modules and develop a database structure.

Michelle knew staff would want features to make their job easier but, simultaneously, demand that the system was intuitive and easy to learn and use. They'd demand uncluttered screens – then complain when that meant more 'clicks' to choose options from sub-menus. The client would complain about any additional costs – even if they arose because of revised instructions.

Fortunately, the implementation of the new system was dependent on the construction of the corporate headquarters; and that wasn't due to be completed until the end of the year allowing plenty of time for development of the different modules, testing and resolving any bugs – then, in all probability, going through at least a couple of iterations as correcting problems in one area caused issues elsewhere.

Michelle accepted such demands as part of her job. Finding solutions or negotiating compromises was what she was paid for. Much of the time it felt like she was always under pressure to get things done and answer queries – then there would be long periods waiting for work to be completed. A typical case of 'hurry up and wait'.

She was more concerned about her imminent second consultation with the gender clinic. As far as she could see, everything was proceeding according to plan – but there were always the 'what ifs'. What if her latest blood tests showed a reaction to the hormones? What if the consultant didn't think she was doing enough to progress her transition? Though she couldn't see how much more she could do.

She knew, from discussions on Facebook groups she'd joined anonymously, this was just normal nervousness that most trans women went through at this stage. She knew too, that the concerns generally proved unfounded and sessions usually went well. But still …

Glancing at her watch, she saw she had twenty minutes before her online appointment so she switched on the coffee maker then booted up her laptop. Kicking off her heels, she settled in front of the screen, took a sip of the coffee then clicked the link for the Zoom session.

Fiona's picture appeared on the screen next to her – then they became live videos.

"Good evening, Michelle, how are you?"

"I'm fine thanks – how about yourself?"

"Yes, fine. So, how are things going? Have you noticed any changes since starting hormones?"

"Everything seems to be going well. Everything's OK at work. The project I'm managing is on track and I have a good team working for me. No negative reactions to the hormones – and my breasts have started to develop. At the moment, they're like two fried eggs but still noticeably different to before I started HRT. My hips and bum seem to be a bit bigger – presumably that's due to body fat being redistributed." Michelle had no intention of revealing her concerns about the mystery money.

"You mentioned last time you planned to have facial surgery?"

"Yes, I had some work done just before Christmas. It went well and the bruising has now gone."

"I thought you looked a bit different but I wondered if it was a new hair style – or just my memory. You certainly do look very feminine."

"Thank you – though to judge from some of the forums online, you'd think it was a crime to try to make oneself as feminine as possible. Some trans people seem to think It reinforces gender stereotypes and we should live with what we've got."

"What do you think of that viewpoint?"

"If others want to go that route, it's fine with me. Personally, I want to blend in as far as I can. I don't want to constantly carry the flag. I guess that makes me selfish but I just want to get on with my life as Michelle."

After a few minutes, Fiona wound up the consultation.

"OK, Michelle. Everything seems to be on track so I suggest we make another appointment for three months. Does 20th April suit you?"

"Yes, that's fine Fiona. See you then." With that, Michelle clicked on the 'exit' button, entered the next appointment on her calendar then closed down her laptop.

The next three months slipped by without any major incidents. The development of the new system was going well; problems arose, of course, but Michelle managed them as she was paid to do. Even Craig Mann struggled to find reasons to complain about progress.

She joined the team most Friday evenings for drinks and a meal afterwards though she avoided going out to the gay village again with Zoë – who had found herself a boyfriend and no longer invited Michelle to join her.

Nobody had been in touch with her over the Liechtenstein bank account, which she left completely untouched. She hadn't responded to the statement – not that she'd be expected to.

After living in role for six months, everything seemed totally normal for her as Michelle. The only anomalies were seeing what lay between her legs – and having to undergo laser electrolysis. The fried eggs she'd described to Fiona now filled an A cup and Michelle had replaced the original falsies with a smaller version as she no longer needed as much padding.

She had her third consultation with Fiona the week after Easter.

Once again, Fiona was happy with the progress Michelle had made and the way she'd settled into her new life.

"Have you given any thought to where to go for surgery, Michelle?" she'd asked.

"Almost certainly Bangkok, I'm hearing excellent reports of work over there."

"Very true – though I gather they expect you to stay in Thailand for a month afterwards as the procedure is somewhat more invasive."

"That's not a problem. I've been thinking of making a long holiday of it – have a look at the River Kwai. My great-grandfather was a Prisoner of War working on the death railway out there sadly he was one of those who died. One of thousands. Perhaps I'll go on to Australia afterwards."

"That sounds exciting, I'm quite jealous," Fiona told her. "I see no reason why we shouldn't be able to provide a referral after your next appointment – with a view to surgery from October."

"That's brilliant. I'll certainly get things moving."

After agreeing the date for the next consultation, they finished the session. Instead of closing down her laptop, she clicked on a link to the hospital in Bangkok and pulled up the enquiry form. She then picked up her mug of coffee but, discovering that the last quarter had gone cold while on the Zoom session, took the mug into the kitchen, tipped the dregs away and was about to make a fresh brew when she decided it called for something celebratory. Opening the fridge, she took out a bottle of Prosecco and poured a glass.

Chapter 24. A4E: Deniability

You're absolutely certain that Nathan Poulson can't be traced back to us, Tommy?" Peter Holmes, Leader of Action 4 England, demanded as smoke from his cigar spiralled towards the ceiling.

"I don't see how, Peter. His isn't on our membership lists and the only time we met him was at the Nelson Arms. He may have been observed at a meeting or a rally – but that applies to hundreds of others. Why?"

"I had a phone call from Ian Davidson, that Sergeant at Islington. Apparently, they've worked out the explosion wasn't caused by Islamic extremists but it was made to look that way."

"Have they identified Poulson?"

"Not so far. But it seems they've shown his DNA is mainly South Eastern English but with some Celtic and Balkan – but no Arab."

"OK, so that contradicts the documentation we provided him – but it still doesn't identify him specifically. If they had his DNA on record, they'd already know who he was – same if they could do it through dental records or any other methods. They might conclude that he was linked to a group like ours – but they can't prove a connection to A4E."

"I'm sure you're right, Tommy. And, even if they did, we wouldn't know anything about the explosion."

"Of course not, Peter. Just an overzealous and misguided sympathiser who went far beyond what we would do."

"There's no possibility of anything Poulson left behind incriminating us?"

"No. Even if they identify him and find where he lived, his flat has been relet for more than six months – the council will have cleared it out before allocating it to a new tenant. They may even have redecorated it. So, if there had been any A4E material it would have been removed and destroyed."

Chapter 25. Ali: Tracing the Bomber

The sign on Khalid Ali's door at the Habbani Embassy in London's Mayfair district read 'Assistant Trade Secretary' but his duties had little to do with trade – other than of information. The news he'd received from a young Police Officer tasked with mundane duties filing reports for the team investigating the attack on the train last October had been very interesting. DNA testing had identified the attacker as European, probably an Englishman.

He'd been certain it hadn't been an Arab, if it had, his sources in the various groups would have informed him. It might have been Mossad trying to cause difficulties but that seemed unlikely. A racist group was much more likely. Ali contacted his network of informers across the UK – some of whom might tell him things they'd withhold from the police. He also checked his list of known or suspected members of racist groups and sympathisers – with particular interest in any with experience of explosives.

He was angered by the attempt to lay the blame for the atrocity on Arabs – and was determined to ensure that those responsible were punished for their actions. If he had his way, that punishment would go beyond any that a British Court might inflict. Even a whole life sentence in Belmarsh prison would not be sufficient for the blasphemy of condemning true believers for the attack. But first, he had to identify those who were culpable. He had no doubt that SO15, the Metropolitan Police Counter Terrorism Command, would be taking similar steps – but would they try as hard as he would to correct the impression that Arabs had been culpable?

Chapter 26. Michelle: Time to Fly

Michelle turned to the members of the Project Board.

"Any questions?" she asked.

She'd just concluded her final report for the second phase of the project. The modules had been developed and tested and had completed their user acceptance last week; the database test migrations had, eventually, been successful from all three systems used by the different parts of the business. The components for the datacentre to be installed at the new corporate headquarters were on order – as were the desktop terminals and all the printers. Training had been scheduled for the new year to tie in with the commissioning of the new system.

"I haven't any questions, do you Craig, or you Sylvia?" Robert Nicholls asked the other members of the board.

The client's Project Manager, Craig Mann reluctantly shook his head.

"No, none."

Sylvia smiled, "Nor me."

"Well, Michelle, I have to say you did a fantastic job. As far as I can see, you've achieved all of the initial objectives within the planned timeframe and, most incredibly, within budget when we allow for changes made at our request. Well done."

"Yes, Sir Robert, I wholeheartedly concur," agreed Sylvia. "It's been a textbook example of how to manage a project. And I'm going to take some of the credit for having recruited you for the role," she added with a smile.

Michelle had to hide a grin of her own as it hadn't actually been her that Sylvia had interviewed over Zoom. Would the other

Michelle have handled the project as well? Who knew? But it didn't matter in any case.

"So, Michelle, I gather you're taking a break now until the implementation phase starts at the end of January?" the client's managing director enquired.

"I am, Sir Robert. I'm off for a tour of South East Asia and Australia. It's an area I've wanted to explore for some time. The planning is all sorted for the hardware roll out and there's nothing for me to do in the interim. It's not a long enough hiatus to do another project so it's a convenient point to take an extended holiday." Michelle replied.

"Sounds quite an adventure. I'm sure you'll enjoy it and I look forward to hearing about your experiences when you get back. When do you leave?"

"Wednesday. I'm flying via Amsterdam. It gives me tomorrow to finalise any paperwork in the office."

With that, Michelle smiled at Robert Nicholls and gathered up her documents.

On the Wednesday, Michelle emptied her fridge, disposed of any other perishables, cleaned the kitchen surfaces, unplugged all electrical devices and turned the thermostat application down to a minimum before leaving for the airport. It would be ten weeks before she'd be back in the flat.

She could hardly believe this day had finally arrived. It was just over a year since that fateful train crash and the opportunity to take on Michelle's identity. Now, in a few days, she'd have undergone surgery that would correct the flawed genitalia she'd been born with. She tried not to feel too excited by the prospect – events could still conspire against her.

A new outbreak of Covid could have stopped her travelling – but any prohibitions usually came with a few days' notice so, hopefully, that wouldn't happen.

One of her flights could be delayed – but she'd built nearly 48 hours contingency into her schedule.

She could fall ill or have an accident – but she felt fine at the moment and would take care to avoid injury.

There'd been no further contact over the mysterious bank account; but, even so, she'd booked her flights through Amsterdam to avoid going anywhere near Dubai – just in case. Her first flight was at twenty to two, via KLM. It was a short hop but she'd booked business class as it doubled her baggage allowance and the extra cost was minimal compared with the overall cost of her trip. After a short stop at Schiphol, she'd be on the second, longer, leg to Bangkok's Suvarnabhumi airport. They were due in Bangkok at ten to two in the afternoon after the overnight flight.

Despite the life-changing surgery she was about to have – and the risks entailed in any operation – she was calm and quickly fell asleep on the business class lie-flat seat after a late dinner and glass of Champagne.

By the time she woke six hours later, the Boeing 777 was flying south of the Himalayas with peaks, one of which, she assumed, was Mount Everest, visible on the horizon. She took out her phone and took a photograph. Looking at the in-flight magazine, she noticed that the usual route from Amsterdam to Bangkok went north of the mountain range. Presumably, this had been changed to pass south of Ukraine and Russian territory.

Settling her seat upright, Michelle made her way to the washroom to freshen up and change. Back at her seat the cabin crew asked what she'd like for breakfast and brought it to her a few minutes later. She hadn't long finished her coffee when the chimes rang to draw attention to the 'fasten seat belts' sign illuminating.

The waters of the Bay of Bengal gave way to the coast and forests of Myanmar as the aircraft commenced its descent into Bangkok. Michelle felt the aircraft slow and the already muted sound of the engines diminished further. Outside the windows, whisps of clouds quickly gave way to a denser fog. That, in turn, cleared, revealing a spider's web of roads, houses, apartment blocks and factories. As it became possible to make out individual vehicles speeding along the motorways or caught in the gridlocked roads, the Boeing banked to starboard limiting her view through the window next to her to the sky. There was a jerk as the pilot lowered the flaps and undercarriage.

Although not afraid of flying, Michelle knew landing was one of the most dangerous periods of any flight. She recalled the adage 'A good landing is one you can walk away from; a great landing is one where you can use the aircraft again'.

As the 777 came closer to the ground, she estimated the remaining height by the details you could make out. She'd thought they were at about two hundred feet when they crossed a motorway; then the threshold of the runway passed underneath them and there was the screech as the tyres hit the tarmac and the roar as the pilot activated the thrust reversers to use the engines to slow the aircraft.

The runway markers flashing past the window slowed as the brakes took effect and the aircraft turned off the runway and taxied up to their designated gate. Ground staff scurried around – a bowser arrived to top up the fuel for the next leg to Hong Kong; luggage carts drew up along with cleaning vehicles and the honey wagon ready to empty the human sewage stored during the last twelve hours.

Once the fasten seat belt signs were extinguished, Michelle stood up and collected her cabin bag.

Thanking the crew as she stepped onto the air bridge, she swallowed deeply. Her passport contained the original Michelle's biometric data based on the photograph. She'd compared the measurements and, as far as she could see, there were minimal differences since her facial surgery. Her hair hid the shape of her ears; her eyes were blue – the same as her predecessor and she'd taken care with her make-up to shade and shape her appearance.

Hopefully, if any discrepancies were noticed, the facial surgery she'd undergone would be an adequate explanation. She had the receipt from the hospital with her and Michelle's birth certificate. Nevertheless, there was a risk that she'd be refused entry and that would wreck her plans.

The queue shuffled along as the border officer dealt with the row of incoming passengers. Eventually, it was Michelle's turn. She passed over her passport.

Chapter 27. Ali: Identity Revealed

Ali looked at the spreadsheet on his laptop. He'd whittled down the original list of known members of racist groups, including those who weren't officially members but had been seen at meetings and rallies – removing those who'd been seen since the train attack, any still active on social media, individuals in prison or recorded as having died.

There were seven names remaining.

There was no guarantee any of them were the bomber – but one of them *could* be. It was, in any case, the only lead he was left with. None of his contacts had come up with any other information about which group had been behind the explosion.

If he could identify the bomber, it should lead to the organisation responsible.

He lit a cigarette; the Habban embassy north of Hyde Park was sovereign territory so not subject to British law prohibiting smoking at work.

Ali had photographs of the possible suspects. Two of those were poor quality from crowd shots on the internet - but they would have to suffice. More in hope than with any confidence, he emailed copies to his network asking if anyone had information about the movements of the suspects in the three days prior to the atrocity.

Amar Singh, sitting in the cramped office at the back of his shop on the other side of the city, read the email from Khalid Ali and looked at the photographs. Enquiring about events from nearly a year ago was asking a lot – but he did recall an incident; and one of the photographs could be the man who'd marched past his shop and showed utter distaste as he did so. It had stuck in his mind as the man's demeanour contrasted with the usual local residents. Instead of dirty hoodies, torn jeans and trainers and roll-ups dangling from lips, he clearly took pride in his appearance. His shoes had been polished and his charcoal grey trousers had been pressed to produce knife-edge creases. Even without the blazer with a regimental badge and matching tie, Amar had recognised the military bearing. He'd served himself in the RAF – rising to the rank of Warrant Officer.

Although he didn't share Ali's religion, Amar Singh was happy to provide any information that came his way about racist groups. They had their fair share in his location – and, if they were Islamaphobes, they were also likely to object to his own presence. He'd experienced low-level problems from customers of the Nelson's Arms and had set up CCTV to cover the front of his shop from both directions. It ran 24/7, recording onto a hard drive usually overwriting the recordings after a few days. He'd been upgrading the system the morning the individual had walked past. The old recorder was still in his store room, kept as a spare – and still had the recordings from that day.

Khalid Ali examined the video extracts Singh had emailed him. In the first two, Poulson was clearly seen walking towards the shop then holding his breath and grimacing as he passed – before moving out of the first camera to the second where the back view showed him crossing the road towards the Nelson's Arms. The second set of videos, recorded some minutes later, were even more revealing. They showed Poulson coming from the direction of the pub with another man. Ali took a screenshot of the second man and ran it through his database.

After a short time, the screen showed a list of a dozen photographs from his files matching the image.

He lit a cigarette then leaned back in his chair.

"So, my friend. You were seen with Tommy James from Action for England twenty-four hours before the attack – was that a coincidence? I doubt it. Now, was Peter Holmes also involved?"

Ali picked up his phone and called Amar Singh.

"Thank you for the videos. They were very revealing. I'm emailing you another photograph; can you see if that individual appears from the same direction? Probably no more than an hour or so later?" he asked.

While waiting for Amar to call back, Khalid Ali searched the internet for information about Action 4 England to bring his records up to date.

His computer signalled the arrival of a new email just as his phone rang.

"I've checked the video – Peter Holmes left the Nelson's Arms and took a cab fifteen minutes after Tommy James and the mystery man," Singh told him. "I've sent you a video showing him."

"Excellent work. You recognised Holmes and James then?"

"Of course; Holmes isn't exactly low profile, is he?"

"True, well, thanks for your help."

After ending the call, Ali viewed the video. There was no question that he'd established a connection between a known racist group and an individual who had disappeared after the attack on the train. It wouldn't stand up in British court – but it was enough to convince him.

Chapter 28. Michelle: Arrival in Bangkok

Michelle stood nervously while the Immigration Officer examined her passport. He looked at her, then down at the passport, shuffled through a few pages, then handed it back.

"Enjoy your visit to Thailand, madam." With that, his attention switched to the next passenger in line. Michelle breathed again as she tucked the passport into her bag; her legs felt like jelly as she turned towards the baggage hall. There was no sign yet of the luggage from her flight so she found the ladies' toilets and sat down in a cubicle.

She closed her eyes, tilted her head backwards and took several deep breaths. As her heart rate returned to normal, Michelle took hold of her penis and aimed it downwards. Another few days and she wouldn't need to do that ever again – she'd be rid of that offensive appendage. After wiping herself, she pulled up her knickers, smoothed her skirt down and flushed the pan. After washing her hands, she touched up her make-up and ran a comb through her hair.

Back at the carousel, she watched her bag fall onto the track and waited for it to reach her.

After customs, she followed signs for the exit. As she stepped outside the terminal building, she was assaulted by the hot and humid atmosphere – a huge contrast to the air-conditioned capsules she'd been in for the last thirty or so hours.

A little over an hour later, she opened the door to her hotel room, dropped her case at the end of the bed then looked around. The room was light and airy, the décor mainly white walls and light-coloured wood panelling with views from the large windows over rooftops to the sea. She tested the mattress for firmness – then decided to take a nap.

Suitably refreshed, Michelle showered and put on a light cotton sleeveless dress in a blue and pink geometric pattern before making her way to the restaurant. She was greeted by a young woman in traditional dress who bowed with her hands together; Michelle returned the gesture and followed her to a table. She looked around the room – she seemed to be the only one on her own. Most of the other tables had mixed couples or groups of two women together. She wondered if she was the only patient from the clinic – or, if there were others in the hotel, perhaps they were eating elsewhere.

After dinner, she took a stroll down the main road. The sun had set, the oppressive heat and humidity had given way to a more comfortable temperature. Tuk-tuks, mopeds and scooters puttered along the road – fighting for space with the Toyota, Hyundai, Nissans and Honda cars and pick-ups. Hundreds of power cables were strung along both sides of the highway and across the carriageways – Michelle wondered how they could be serviced and how often they might short-circuit.

Returning to the hotel, she decided to have a drink in the bar. Ordering a glass of white wine, she sat on a sofa next to a window giving a view over the city.

"Do you mind if I join you?" asked a tall, well-built woman who had approached her table. "We seem to be the only ones on our own – or, perhaps you're waiting for someone to join you?"

"No, I'm not waiting for anyone – do sit down," Michelle answered. She judged the other individual to be in her late forties or early fifties.

"Thank you, I do hate drinking on my own. I'm Suzanne, by the way," the visitor remarked.

"Nice to meet you, Suzanne, I'm Michelle."

"So, Michelle, what brings you to Bangkok? If you don't mind me asking. Are you on holiday or business?"

Michelle paused before answering. She was quite certain that Suzanne was here for the same reason as herself. But did she want to reveal her purpose? She'd taken a lot of care to separate Michelle's identity from Jeff's and to conceal the fact that Michelle was transgender. The clinic had to know, of course, but she wanted to limit how far her secret was spread."

"Oh, mainly a holiday," she said, sidestepping the question. "What about you?"

"I came here for a medical procedure. I'm transgender and had genital reconstruction surgery, a few days ago. The clinic recommended this hotel." Suzanne seemed to stare at Michelle, challenging her to react.

"Is that right?" Michelle replied, picking up her glass and lifting it in Suzanne's direction in a toast. "I hope it went well."

"Thank you. It did. I take it you're British, I'm from South Africa, Durban. Have you ever been there?"

"Yes, I'm English – I live in Manchester and, no, I haven't been to South Africa. It's on my bucket list though."

"You should come, it has whatever you might want for a holiday – wildlife in the Kruger, Table Mountain at the Cape, scenery, great beaches; wine tours. Some great diving around Durban, you name it."

"The wine tours sound good but I'm not sure about the diving, particularly around Great White Sharks. Have you been to Manchester?"

"Not yet. My surgery cost a lot – so all my spare cash has gone into that. It's taken me seven years to get the money together – it hasn't helped that the costs have kept going up. Still, it's done now. I just have to stay in Bangkok for a few more days so I can be monitored."

Michelle felt guilty not sharing her own story. Could it hurt to share with someone who lived eight thousand miles from her? It might well be useful to get some first-hand information from someone who'd been through the op.

Chapter 29. A4E: Southern Tour

Tommy James sat down with Peter Holmes.

"Have you time for an update on the tour arrangements, Peter?"

"Absolutely, how's it going?"

"Pretty much sorted. We leave Heathrow on the 14th December – direct Virgin flight to Johannesburg where we're staying with the Bekkers at their private game reserve near Phalaborwa. Arnou has invited representatives from around the Transvaal to meet us. As well as the discussions, he's laid on a day's hunting."

Holmes nodded his head and smiled at the thought of shooting some game. He had little time for the namby-pambies who thought hunting should be outlawed.

"Sounds good."

"We then return to Jo'burg and fly Qantas to Sydney. We have three days of meetings in the Sydney area – seems that there's a turf war between some of the groups and they refuse to attend the same events."

"Jesus, don't they realise there are bigger battles to be fought than fighting between ourselves? Bloody idiots," remarked Holmes shaking his head in sorrow.

"I know. It's insane – but we have to work with what we've got. Anyway, we then have a break for Christmas. We've been invited to spend it with the Baileys on their station between Sydney and Canberra."

James looked at Holmes to see if he had any questions. Holmes indicated that he should continue with the briefing.

"After Christmas, we fly to Melbourne, then Adelaide and Brisbane for further meetings – then back to Sydney for the flight to New Zealand. We have more meetings in Wellington and Auckland before returning to Sydney for our flight back to London via Singapore."

"All sounds very good. And costly."

"It is. But the reaction to the train bombing pulled in plenty and our hosts on this trip are providing accommodation and paying a fee for your talks. We won't quite break even on the trip but the contacts should be worthwhile. I'm also inviting donations on the website towards the expense of the trip."

"OK, Tommy. Now, just to confirm, the flights are all on white Commonwealth country airlines, aren't they?

"Of course. We can't guarantee the race of their staff, though."

"No, I realise that – just so long as the airlines aren't likely to expect us to eat ethnic junk – and the flights avoid any stopovers in the Middle East."

Chapter 30. Ali: Planning Interception

Khalid Ali looked at the announcement on A4E's website that Holmes and James were planning what they described as liaison visits to South Africa, Australia and New Zealand. It wasn't likely they'd transit through any Middle Eastern hubs where they might be detained for questioning – at least, they wouldn't do so deliberately.

Calling in a favour, he obtained details of their flights and realised there could be an opportunity. He picked up the secure telephone on his desk and dialled. The call was routed via scrambling devices that made interception difficult.

At the other end of the call, Colonel Viraj Malik, his senior, looked out of his window, over Shajdad City to the desert beyond.

He listened to Ali's report and suggestions and, after a moment's thought, agreed to look into the feasibility of Ali's plan.

Stroking his beard, he sipped from a cup of coffee while he pondered who was best placed to provide the information they needed.

Chapter 31. Michelle: Surgery

On the morning before she was due to have surgery, Michelle packed an overnight bag with items she'd need in the hospital and secured the rest in her main suitcase which she'd leave at the hotel.

After checking in she was shown to her room. It could easily have passed for a three- or four-star hotel room if it wasn't for the medical monitors. Next to the bed were a visitor's chair and a locker for her bits and pieces – not that she'd be having any visitors. She walked over to the window and looked out over the city's roofscape. She was here. Her dreams were about to come true – only a disaster could surely stop the surgery from happening now. Her thoughts were interrupted by a nurse entering her room.

"Michelle? My name is Bussaba, can I please check your date of birth?" she asked.

"Twenty-fourth November nineteen eighty-five," Michelle confirmed as the nurse checked it against her records.

"Thank you. I'm afraid I have to give you this laxative to clear out your bowels ready for surgery. It is potent – so I suggest you don't wander too far from the bathroom after taking it. You'll be given a further dose this evening. As you know, you are not allowed any food or drink other than water now until after your surgery."

With that, Bussaba handed Michelle the dose of pink liquid. Wrinkling her nose, she drank it – then waited for it to take effect. The nurse had not been exaggerating about the potency and Michelle felt quite drained by the time it had done its job.

There was little for her to do that afternoon and evening between doses of laxative and visits by the anaesthetist and surgeon. Knowing she would be confined to bed for several days, she sat in the chair and read a book on her tablet.

Once she was certain the second dose of laxative had finished flushing out her bowels, Michelle took a shower – the last she'd be able to have for nearly a week – then got ready for bed. She'd wondered if she would get any sleep the night before surgery or if she'd lie awake tossing and turning; thinking about the operation. But she was strangely detached about what the next day would bring.

If it went well, then all would be fine. If something went wrong, she'd either survive or not. If she didn't, she wouldn't be around to worry. If she did survive after a problem – then the most likely issues, she thought, were a heart problem or brain damage. The former would probably demand changes to her lifestyle – the latter might leave her unaware of what was happening to her. She couldn't influence any of those outcomes now so there was no point worrying.

"Michelle. Michelle. Can you hear me?"

The question broke through the fog engulfing her brain. She opened her eyes, blinking several times. Bussaba was standing by her bedside, smiling.

"Welcome back, Michelle. How are you feeling?"

"Groggy."

"That's to be expected. You're back on the ward now – your operation went well; the surgeon was very pleased. She'll be along later to speak to you. Are you in any pain?"

Michelle thought about it.

"No. No pain, just a bit uncomfortable."

"Well, if you do feel any pain, let us know and we'll give you something for it."

"Now, you can lift your shoulders slightly but mustn't move your torso; and please keep your legs apart and don't cross them as that could risk DVTs. OK?"

She woke again sometime later – she had no idea how long – to find Dr Huang, her surgeon, standing there.

"How are you feeling? Michelle," she asked.

"Sleepy. But happy. Thank you."

"No pain still?"

"No, as I told Bussaba, I feel uncomfortable – but I wouldn't call it pain."

"That's good. I'm very pleased to say that the operation went very well; no hitches and you should end up with a satisfactory vagina and urethra and sensitive clitoris and g-spot. Provided, that is, you follow instructions about keeping it clean and dilated. I'll see you again in a few days."

"Thank you," Michelle answered with a smile.

The next five days were tedious but just had to be endured. All she could do was lie virtually immobile. She was able to use her tablet to read, to access the internet and look up places on her itinerary after leaving hospital. No doubt if her colleagues had been aware of her real reason for visiting Thailand, she'd have had messages of support and might have chatted to them over the web but she'd kept off social media in case someone from Michelle's schooldays tried to find all of their old classmates.

When Dr Huang returned a few days later to check on the healing process, she declared herself satisfied and, after drains and catheters had been removed, allowed Michelle to get out of bed and have a shower.

After nearly a week on her back, Michelle was quite unsteady at first but made it into the en-suite bathroom. She pulled off her nightdress and looked at herself in the full-length mirror. The image that looked back at her no longer had any link to Jeff. She was now simply Michelle. A woman with the body she should have been born with.

Chapter 32. Ali: Palace Approval

Colonel Viraj Malik read the email he'd received. He stared at the computer screen while he picked up the cup of coffee next to his keyboard and took a sip of the dark liquid. He swivelled his chair so he could look out of the window. The Royal Palace, source of his email, dominated the skyline. To his right, the minaret of the nearby mosque reminded him that the muezzin would be calling the faithful to Asr prayers shortly. He did, however, have time to call Khalid Ali in London before preparing for his devotional duties.

Khalid Ali picked up the white handset before the second ring had died away. There was no reason for him to wonder who was calling. The phone was a dedicated secure line to his superior. He could imagine Colonel Malik looking out of his window at a sunlit scene – while rain rattled against the windows of his own office.

"Khalid Ali," he announced.

"Ali, your suggestion of intercepting Holmes and James has been approved by the Palace. You are to handle the mission."

"Thank you, Colonel. I won't let you down."

"There are still several weeks before the targets leave for South Africa but I want you here as soon as possible. You are to prepare plans to cover all potential alternatives. Now the Emir has given his approval, it is imperative that you are successful. Failure is not an option."

Ali realised that this mission would either establish his career or see the end of it.

"Yes, Colonel. I will hand over my other projects here and catch the first available flight."

Chapter 33. Michelle: Convalescence

Michelle packed her small suitcase then had a final look around the accommodation that had been her home for the past week.

Nurse Bussaba came into the room.

"Are you ready, Michelle?"

"I think so, thanks for everything and please thank the other members of staff for me, will you?"

"Of course. Now, here are some painkillers just in case you need them. Don't forget, keep everything clean and dilate regularly. Take things gently for the next couple of weeks and don't be too impatient to try out your new equipment for real."

"Don't worry, I won't. I'm at the hotel here for a few days then I've got a car booked to take me to Pattaya where I plan to just relax around the pool – at least my bikini will fit properly now."

"It sounds wonderful. Now, let me take your case for you."

With that, Bussaba took the handle of the small wheeled cabin bag leaving Michelle to slip her handbag strap over her shoulder. They walked down the corridor before taking the lift to the ground-floor reception.

Outside, an earlier shower had stopped and any evidence of the rain was evaporating from the roads and pavements. The temperature was already in the mid-twenties and Michelle was grateful for the taxi's air-conditioning even for the short ride to the hotel.

After re-registering, she arranged for the case she'd left there the previous week to be taken to her room together with the cabin bag – then walked through into the bar for a glass of Prosecco to celebrate her operation. The lunch buffet caught her eye and she decided to have some Pla Neung Manow – steamed fish with a lime and chilli sauce. Her digestive system was still recovering from its enforced abstinence after surgery. No doubt that would be reflected in her weight.

As she was eating, she looked around the dining room wondering if there were any other residents waiting to see Dr Huang or, like herself, recuperating from surgery. This was, after all, the hotel the clinic recommended.

After people-watching for a few minutes and finishing her meal and glass of wine, she knew she couldn't put off the inevitable any longer.

It was time for her mid-day dilation session. Four times a day, she had to spend an hour inserting several sizes of plastic dilators ranging from about two to four centimetres diameter and from nine to sixteen centimetres long into her neo-vagina to prevent it from closing up. It was an uncomfortable and messy exercise calling for generous quantities of lubricant. Including preparation and cleaning up afterwards, each session took nearly an hour.

'If it wasn't such a clinical procedure,' she thought, *"it might be quite enjoyable – she certainly felt some sensations and, let's face it, lots of women used similar devices to pleasure themselves.'*

She'd been instructed to do very little the first couple of weeks after surgery. Even walking any significant distance took it out of her so she needed to gradually re-build her stamina and muscle strength. As the week in the hotel slipped by, she found sitting down became easier and she could manage walking for an hour or more without becoming too tired. She was thankful that her regular exercise regime before coming out to Thailand meant she was fit. Even so, she kept to her original plan of leaving visiting the main tourist attractions around Bangkok until later in her tour and limited herself to a few short boat trips from the hotel's own jetty.

Seven days after being discharged, she visited the clinic again for a check-up.

"How have you been, Michelle?" Dr Huang enquired.

"Fine, thank you. Sitting was a bit uncomfortable at first and I tired quickly but I've been gradually increasing the distance I walk each day."

"Yes, very good. Any pain or bleeding or any other discharge?"

"None at all."

"Fine, well hop up onto the couch and I'll just have a look."

"Excellent," Huang remarked after checking her handiwork. "Everything looks perfectly fine. I believe that you are going to the beach then doing a bit of a tour of the River Kwai before returning to Bangkok."

"Yes, that's right," Michelle confirmed.

"Fine, well, enjoy your trip – don't forget to avoid overtiring yourself or doing anything that puts pressure on your groin for the time being. I'll see you again in a couple of weeks for a final check."

The following morning, Michelle checked out of the hotel – reminding reception that she would be returning in three weeks for one night. Her driver was waiting for her and took the cases she pointed out to him and put them in the boot of the white Toyota parked outside.

He then held the rear door open for her to get in.

"I'll sit in the front, if you don't mind, I want to be able to recline the seat," she told the driver.

"Very good, madam," he replied.

The drive was through flat countryside with industry encroaching near the road and farmland beyond for much of the way. As in the city, all electrical services were provided via overhead cables strung between poles – literally dozens at any time it seemed. Clearly, the Thais didn't bury their cables. Michelle was also bemused by the fact that Thais drove on the left-hand side of the road – though it hadn't ever been part of the British Empire which was the usual reason for driving on the left.

South of Chonburi, the horizon ahead was broken by hillier country while the main highway remained on the flat coastal plain.

By the time she arrived at her hotel in Pattaya, Michelle was glad the journey was over. Her nether regions felt numb and it was a great relief to stretch her legs.

A porter came to the car and took her case into the reception area while she paid and tipped the driver.

In her room, her priority was the obligatory dilation; then she realised that would have to wait until she'd dealt with an even more pressing need.

Her task completed, she applied factor fifty suntan lotion, put on a skimpy, multi-coloured, bikini that concealed next to nothing then slipped on a matching kaftan top; a floppy hat and sunglasses and her tablet loaded with books. The bedrooms were in small groups between the main lobby area and the beach with pathways winding between ponds and islands of vegetation with palm trees providing shade. She wandered through the grounds and found a bar overlooking the smooth sandy beach and the teal waters gently breaking on the shoreline. Overhead, birds screeched in the brilliant azure sky.

Choosing a Blue Hawaiian cocktail to match the scene, Michelle removed her top and stretched out on a lounger. She couldn't resist looking at the small triangles of material covering her breasts and between her legs. Her breasts had expanded to a 'B' cup which suited her frame; her hips were about an inch larger and she'd kept her waist in trim with a combination of diet and exercise. No evidence now remained of how her body had looked before that day just over a year ago when the train crash had presented a once-in-a-lifetime opportunity. Nor, for that matter, of how her life had been. Losing touch with her daughters had been hard and, no doubt, every one of their birthdays and Christmases would bring painful reminders. But there was no doubt in her mind that she'd made the right choice.

She sipped her cocktail and looked around. A man, apparently on his own, sitting on a lounger further along the row, smiled at her then lifted his glass as if to say 'cheers'. Michelle tilted her head and returned the gesture. He stood up and walked over to her.

"Hi, do you speak English?" he enquired in an American accent.

"Possibly better than you as I *am* English and I'm guessing you're American," Michelle told him with a smile.

"Touché," he responded. "May I join you?" He gestured at the free lounger next to her.

"Be my guest."

"I'm Clifford Miller, Cliff to my friends. Are you here on vacation?"

"Nice to meet you, Cliff. I'm Michelle. Yes, I'm on holiday. How about yourself?"

"I say vacation, you say holiday; tomayto; tomahto. OK, yes, I get your point, Michelle," he answered with a twinkle in his eye.

Michelle found the way Cliff laughed at himself interesting. No, interesting wasn't the word. Attractive. She found him attractive – not just his looks but his whole demeanour. That realisation surprised her. She'd never been attracted to men before; she'd always identified as heterosexual when living as a male and had never considered sex with men.

While living as Michelle and preparing for surgery, she'd wondered if that would remain the case. Whether she'd continue to be attracted to women or if transitioning would release some latent orientation towards guys. Now she was getting the first indication that the latter might well be the answer.

She couldn't help wondering as Cliff spoke to her what it would be like to go to bed with him. The problem was that she couldn't have sex for at least three months. On the other hand, there was no harm chatting.

As the sun settled lower over the Gulf of Thailand and the island of Ko Lan, Michelle and Cliff continued to talk and exchange information about their respective trips.

"I was in Bangkok for a few days but only arrived in Pattaya today," Michelle told him.

He, in turn, told her that he'd been at the hotel for nearly a week and was about to move on to Cambodia then Vietnam.

"I'm doing a bike tour of the Ho Chi Minh trail," he told her.

"That sounds quite an adventure, but much too much like hard work and roughing it for me. I like my comforts."

"Well, it could be my last big adventure before I turn fifty. It's kind of been top of my bucket list for a while. What's top of yours?" he asked.

Michelle had to think about the question. Until a year ago it had been to live fully as female; then, until last week, to have surgery. Now those had been achieved, what *did* she want to do?

"Dive the Great Barrier Reef?" she suggested. She wasn't ready to tell someone she'd only just met her real dream was now to find someone to love her as Michelle, maybe even get married.

"So, what's stopping you?"

"Nothing. In fact, I hope to be doing that in a few weeks."

Michelle glanced at her watch and realised that it was time for her session with the plastic tubes and a dollop of lubricant. She gathered up her bag.

"It's been great chatting to you, Cliff. Maybe I'll see you later," she said.

"Would you like to join me for dinner this evening?" he asked.

"That would be lovely," she replied.

"How about meeting about eight at the pool bar?"

"Eight is perfect. See you later."

As she strolled along the path to her room, she glanced back at Cliff who was sitting on his lounger watching her. She smiled as she returned a slight wave of his hand.

After dilating and showering, Michelle looked through her wardrobe for something to wear for her date. She took out some slinky black underwear including a strapless bra – even though she knew that it would be dangerous to let Cliff get far enough to see it. But that wasn't what was important; SHE would feel great knowing she was wearing it.

She sat at the dressing table and applied her make-up, taking care to emphasise her features and blending eye shadow tones that complimented the deep mauve halter neck dress that lay across the bed; matching lipstick completed her appearance. A pair of strappy sandals and a matching evening bag concluded the look.

She stood in front of the full-length mirror and checked herself from various angles.

She would do, she thought. In fact, more than do. She looked - and felt – fabulous. A spritz of YSL Manifesto and she was ready.

Cliff was waiting at the bar as she approached. He stood up from the stool he'd been sitting on and took a few steps towards her; holding out his hands.

"You look incredible, Michelle," he said then leant forward to lightly kiss her cheek, taking her hands in his.

Michelle could smell his masculine cologne as she let him lead her to the bar.

"What would you like to drink?"

She thought for a moment; making her mind up between wine or a cocktail. Settling for the latter, she looked at the chalked-up list behind the counter.

"Something long and refreshing, I think. Sea Breeze please."

"That sounds good, I'll join you," Cliff responded.

While Cliff placed his order with the barman, Michelle took in his appearance. He wore a light blue open-necked shirt over taupe chinos. He'd obviously shaved before meeting her – his cheek had felt smooth when it brushed against hers. Thank goodness he didn't go for the 'designer stubble' look. As far as she could see, the watch he was wearing wasn't an ostentatious brand like a Rolex though it was quite masculine with various dials on the face. In spite of wearing two- and half-inch heels, she had to look up to see his eyes so he was probably about five foot eleven – some four inches taller than her.

When the barman handed Cliff the chit to sign for the drinks, he let go of Michelle's hand – she hadn't actually registered that he was still holding it.

"There you are, Michelle. Cheers," he said as he handed her one of the cocktails.

Michelle responded "Cheers", as they clinked glasses.

After finishing their Sea Breezes, they left the bar and walked over to the restaurant. As they sauntered through the lush vegetation, they could hear insects chirping away in the bushes surrounding the ponds. Michelle didn't object as Cliff took hold of her hand again.

Once they'd ordered their meal and the waiter had brought a bottle of wine and poured it, Cliff looked across the table.

"You mentioned earlier that you'll be scuba diving on the Great Barrier Reef in a few weeks – is that a separate holiday or are you out this way for a while?" he asked.

Michelle paused to consider just how much to tell him.

"I'm running a major project back in the UK. It's at a point where we've done everything we can until a new building is finished – so I have a few weeks free. Before my current job, I was working in the Gulf States under a lot of pressure and hadn't had a decent holiday for three years; so now I'm making up for lost time. I'm spending about a month here in Thailand then spending a few weeks in Oz, before flying back to the UK."

"Sounds fabulous. Have you dived before?"

"Yes, I did a bit in the Gulf and spent the odd week or so on the Red Sea."

"Do you fancy a dive trip here? We could buddy up."

"Sadly, I can't. I had some surgery before my holiday – which is partly convalescence. I have to limit what I do until the middle of next month and that includes swimming. It means I'm pretty much restricted to relaxing by the pool or gentle walks for the next week or so. But that's better than sitting in my apartment in Manchester."

Technically, she wasn't being untruthful. There were several surgical procedures that would impose similar restrictions. Knowing men as she did, she thought it was unlikely that he would press for further details.

"I see; that's a shame. How does sailing fit into your regime?"

"If you mean dinghy sailing, there'd be too much risk of falling in the water – but a cruiser would be fine. Why? Do you have a boat here?"

"Not personally, but we can charter one from the marina. Have you been sailing before?"

She had to think for a moment about Michelle's real background. There'd been no hint of any sailing as far as she could remember, no mention of it in her CV – but that didn't mean she'd not done any. If she did go sailing with Cliff, it was possible her experience as Jeff would reveal itself.

"I've done a bit around the Solent," she admitted. "A friend had a yacht. He liked to sail whatever the weather – it was fine when the sun shone but I wasn't as keen when it was very windy and raining." It wasn't entirely true; they'd both preferred sailing in more challenging conditions; taking part in Round the Island Races and Cowes Week events as well as cross-channel races – but fitting that into Michelle's backstory would be difficult.

"So, how about it? Shall we take out a sailboat tomorrow?" Cliff pressed.

"Why not, it sounds lovely."

After dinner, they strolled down to the beach. Cliff slipped his arm around Michelle's waist and pulled her close to his side; she reached behind him and let her head rest against his arm.

"Just look at that moon," Michelle remarked turning towards Cliff. "It seems huge; much bigger than at home."

Cliff took her in his arms and bent his head forward. As their lips met, Michelle slid her arms around his neck and responded to his kiss.

She felt her legs giving way under her. Whether it was the passion of the kiss – or the absence of oxygen, she wasn't sure but she pulled her lips away from Cliff's to take a breath. There was no question in her mind now about her sexual orientation as Michelle.

They looked into each other's eyes then fastened their lips together again.

"Shall we go to your room or mine?" Cliff asked.

"I'm sorry but I can't make love – much as I want to," she told him.

"Not the old 'wrong time of month' excuse, surely," he said; his tone tinged with sarcasm, holding onto one of her arms.

"No, not at all. They aren't a problem for me. I told you earlier I had some surgery before coming out here and need to allow it to heal."

"Oh. Right. But you were happy to lead me on and let me buy you dinner and drinks."

"I beg your pardon? You think that meant I was prepared to jump into bed with you for that? Now let me go," she said firmly, dragging herself out of his grip, picking up the hem of her dress and running along the path, half expecting Cliff to chase after her.

Fortunately, he didn't and she reached her room safely, opened the door, stepped inside then leaned against it to close it before turning round and locking it.

She was still shaking with anger as she sat on the bed and removed her shoes. How dare Cliff assume she'd go to bed with him just for a meal? Ironically, if she'd been able to have sex, she would probably have been more than happy to do so. It was his reaction to being turned down that annoyed her. Surely all men weren't like that were they?

It was bad enough that as a trans woman, she risked violence if she wasn't upfront about her history and someone found out about it after having sex and felt they'd been misled. If she also risked abuse for saying no, where did that leave her?

Chapter 34. Ali: Shajdad

Khalid Ali's flight approached the airport in the late afternoon. The runway wasn't long enough for intercontinental airliners – so smaller aircraft were used to link Shajdad, the capital of the Habban Emirate, to hubs in Abu Dhabi and Dubai. The entire country was only about twenty-five miles north to south and twenty east to west.

The original airfield had been built by the RAF to provide a base for patrolling the area and controlling rebel tribes. It had continued in that role until the British left Aden in 1967 after which it was taken over by the local Emir. He used oil revenues to expand the existing facilities into his capital and convert a fortress that stood on a small hill on the northern edge of the city into a modest palace.

As he landed, Ali could see the Emir's citadel off to the right – well away from the flight paths so the royal family wasn't disturbed.

The plane had been less than half full and Ali was soon through immigration but had to wait while the baggage was offloaded and brought to the terminal. He wasn't due at the office until the next morning so took a taxi to his parents' house in the eastern suburbs. As the cab pulled up at his destination, he stopped and gazed at the building for a few moments. His father's twelve-year-old Peugeot sat in the shaded car port at the front of the house. Before he could reach the door, it opened and his mother stood there, her arms opened wide. Behind her, his father waited patiently. Ali dropped his suitcase and stepped into his mother's embrace then greeted his father.

It had been two years since he'd last seen his parents – so he was staying with them for the duration of his time in Shajdad. His sister was a nurse at the main hospital and would be home later, then they could all sit down to a family meal.

The next morning, Ali took his uniform out of the closet. The epaulettes bore the three stars of a captain. If this project went well, he might look forward to promotion to major. At seven o'clock, a taxi pulled up outside the villa to take him to the headquarters of the intelligence service.

The security staff checked his identity card and pass then asked him to wait for an aide from the Intelligence Chief's staff to accompany him.

The first lieutenant saluted Ali who returned the gesture.

"Would you come with me, please, sir?" the aide invited.

Near the end of a corridor on the fifth floor, they entered an office containing four desks. Two were occupied by corporals sitting at computers. A sergeant sat at a third, making a telephone call, while the final desk was currently free. Ali guessed, from the superior quality of the desk and chair, that it was the lieutenant's. Beyond the desks was a door to another office.

The aide knocked on the door then opened it.

"Captain Ali, Sir," he announced before stepping to one side to allow Ali to enter.

Ali strode into the room, came to attention, saluted then greeted his chief.

"As-salamu alaikum, Colonel," he said with a bow.

"Wa-alaikum as-salam, Ali. Come in and sit down," the colonel replied. "Would you like coffee? If so, ask the sergeant to organise it for us, would you?"

Ali stood up again, returned to the door and passed on the colonel's request.

"Now, you suggested somehow intercepting Holmes and James and interrogating them about the train bombing. The question is, how do we intercept them, without causing an international outcry against the emirate? That is what you need to resolve. You will have the support of my private office."

Chapter 35. Michelle on River Kwai

Michelle was bored with just lying by the pool and was relieved to be moving on. She'd followed the clinic's instructions to the letter and had gradually increased her stamina and rebuilt her leg muscles with walks along the beach. The previous day, managing more than a mile without any discomfort. She'd booked a car to take her on the next leg of her trip to Kanchanaburi. It was about a three-and-a-half-hour drive plus any stops they might make en route to allow her to stretch her legs or break for coffee or toilet stops.

Jeff's maternal grandfather had been one of the twelve thousand allied prisoners of war who had died on the 'death railway'. He was buried in the cemetery in Kanchanaburi and Michelle wanted to find his grave and pay her respects to him. She had wondered if there was a risk of exposure by visiting the memorial – but, as thousands of tourists without any personal connections did so every year, she felt it was quite safe. Today was the anniversary of the Japanese attack on Pearl Harbour – so, no doubt, venues would be busier than normal.

The first couple of hours took her back through Bangkok with the road hemmed in for most of the time with industrial and commercial areas. With little to interest her, she reclined the seat to relieve the pressure on her bottom and dozed while the driver guided them through the traffic.

Eventually, they pulled up outside the hotel. Michelle paid and tipped the driver and wished him a safe journey back. She was about to pick up her suitcases when a porter loaded them on a trolley.

"Sawasdee Krab, Khun, are you staying at the hotel?" he asked with the traditional Thai Wai. Michelle did wonder why he'd loaded her cases before checking if she was a resident.

"Sawasdee Ka, yes I am," she replied, putting her own hands together and giving a slight bow.

"Reception is through here. If you register, I will bring your luggage to your room."

After unpacking and carrying out her usual routine, Michelle had a walk down to the River Kwai and the bridge over it. She was disappointed to find it bore no resemblance whatsoever to the structure in the famous film – it was a series of short sections resting on stone pillars; even the surroundings were very different to the film. Instead of stretching across a gorge, the real bridge was at a flat area. She later discovered that the film had been shot in Sri Lanka.

Despite her disappointment, she joined the crowds walking across the bridge and couldn't resist whistling Colonel Bogey, the theme tune from the film. A short walk from the bridge, she had a look round the JEATH War Museum – a poignant display of the brutal conditions endured by the Prisoners of War who worked on the railway.

The next morning, Michelle took a tour that included a trip on the railway along the banks of the river and a visit to the War Cemetery which commemorated nearly seven thousand prisoners of war. She wandered through the rows upon rows of plaques searching for her grandfather's. She found it near the end of one of the rows furthest away from the entrance. She paused and thought about the loss of all of these young men – so many of them in their late teens or early twenties. Neither she nor her mother ever met her maternal grandfather. Her mother had been conceived before her father was shipped overseas and born while he was on a troop ship rounding the Cape of Good Hope. The loss of her grandfather also brought back the loss of her own family. Had that sacrifice been worth it? She certainly hoped it would be. She was now living as she should always have done and that wouldn't have been possible while still with Deborah.

In any case, there was no going back.

She continued along the row of plaques to disguise which, if any of them, had been of particular interest to her then turned back to the entrance to meet the minibus which would return her to the hotel.

After a second night in Kanchanaburi, Michelle checked out of the hotel and was picked up for another stage of her holiday. About an hour north, the coach turned off the main road and down a narrow lane crowded on both sides by dense jungle. It eventually reached a clearing where they stopped with a hiss of the airbrakes. The heat was already building and she was very glad they didn't have to carry their luggage down to a jetty where they were to board 'long-tailed' boats to carry them to the floating hotel further upstream.

The boats were powered by car engines linked directly to the long propellor shafts that gave them their name. Each boat carried about a dozen passengers in six rows of two; the seats barely a couple of inches above the bottom of the hull. Having been pushed off from the jetty, the helmsman opened the throttle and the boat accelerated quickly and was soon skimming over the surface. The shallow draft and propellors meant that they could race through water that wouldn't be deep enough for most craft. They soared around the river bends and over shoals; the spray from the bow occasionally hitting the passengers.

Finally, the helmsman cut the engine and brought the boat alongside a jetty. The hotel comprised a series of rafts moored at the side of the river. Staff on the pontoon helped them out of the boat then showed them to their rooms.

"Please remember there is no electricity at the hotel, you have lanterns for light. The rafts and most of the furniture are made from local bamboo by local Mon villagers. The villagers also provide entertainment for us in the evenings. When you've unpacked and settled in, please come along to the dining room raft where we will serve welcome drinks," one of the staff told them.

As Michelle looked around, she realised this would be a very different experience for her – she couldn't remember when she'd last been unable to access the internet.

Chapter 36. Ali: Mission Authority

So, Captain, are your proposals for bringing Holmes and James to Habban ready for us?" asked Colonel Malik.

"Yes, Sir. With your permission?" Ali replied, indicating the wall-mounted monitor on which the first slide of his PowerPoint presentation was displayed. He glanced around the table at his boss and the representative of the Palace who would judge his plans.

"Just get on with it, Ali."

"Sir. As instructed, I have examined various options for bringing the two infidels to the Emirate in order to interrogate them. According to our information, Holmes and James are booked to fly from London to Johannesburg on the 14th December. They will spend four days at a game reserve for meetings with a local group dedicated to establishing an independent homeland for Boers. They fly on to Australia on the 19th for meetings with white power groups in Sydney, Melbourne, Adelaide and Brisbane and to New Zealand on the 31st – returning to Sydney on the 4th January before taking the Qantas flight via Singapore back to London."

"Yes, Yes! We are familiar with their itinerary. Get on with it!" snapped the man from the Palace.

"Sir! Their outward flight to South Africa takes them over Libya and Chad. I considered intercepting the aircraft in that region and diverting it to Shajdad. However, the runway here is not long enough for the aircraft to land safely and my instructions were to minimise any adverse international repercussions."

"Quite right," Colonel Malik pronounced. "The disappearance of two fascist troublemakers might produce a note or two from the

British Embassy – but they could be ignored. The loss of an aircraft and six hundred passengers would be a different matter."

"Indeed," the man from the Palace agreed. "It would attract attention to the Emirate and might cause questions to be asked. Our American allies would certainly prefer that we avoid interest. We don't want dozens of reporters swarming into Habban – they might stumble across things that we'd prefer to keep hidden. The Americans need their base at Kilometre Eighteen – particularly since they had to close Guantanamo Bay."

"I also considered asking the Libyans or the Chads for the use of one of their airports but any airport large enough to take the aircraft would be too public. Similarly, an overt hi-jacking of the aircraft on their return flight would attract too much attention," Ali continued.

On the screen, a map showed the route the flight would take from London to Johannesburg. This was replaced by maps of Australia and New Zealand.

"I then considered intercepting them while in South Africa, Australia or New Zealand. It's been easy to identify their flights – but not their movements on the ground. We wouldn't know how many local supporters would be on hand so capturing them would be difficult. We don't have special forces 'snatch teams' trained for such work."

"So, how are you going to do it?" demanded the Colonel.

"We will wait until their return flight. The route from Singapore to London will be south of the normal flight path to avoid Russian and Ukrainian airspace. About six hours after departure, it will be approximately 500 nautical miles north of Dubai near the intersection of the borders of Pakistan, Afghanistan and Iran."

"How does that help us?" demanded the man from the Palace. "You've already explained that a hi-jacking is out of the question."

"Very true, Sir. We aren't going to hi-jack the flight." He clicked the control to bring up the next slide.

Chapter 37. Michelle back to Bangkok

I t was soon time for Michelle to leave the floating hotel – taking the long-tailed boat back to the pier where an airconditioned vehicle waited to return her to the capital.

When she first arrived in Bangkok, she'd been focused on her operation and hadn't had time to explore the city. Then, after her discharge, she'd needed to take things gently. Now, four weeks on from surgery, she looked forward to visiting the historic sites such as the Grand Palace, Wat Trimit, with its three-metre-high solid gold statue, and the floating market; maybe even take in some of the fabled night-life.

She still needed to avoid over-taxing herself – and plan her trips around the ever-present dilation sessions – but she felt fine and it would be criminal to miss the opportunity to see some of the famous venues before she returned to the hospital for a final check-up with her surgeon.

Showering that night, she realised that she no longer took time to admire her new body in the mirror or be conscious of any difference in using the loo; it was all just routine and matter of fact.

Chapter 38. A4E Head South

As Michelle travelled back to Bangkok, some six thousand miles away, Peter Holmes and Tommy James arrived at Heathrow Airport for their flight to Johannesburg. By the time they boarded flight VS449 and turned left into the Upper-Class cabin, Michelle was fast asleep. Holmes and James hoped to be able to make good use of the lie-flat seats – after taking advantage of the inclusive champagne; or, to be more accurate, taking advantage of *more* champagne as they'd already had a couple of glasses in the lounge while waiting to board.

Much to Holmes' disgust, the flight attendant responsible for looking after them was Asian. As she returned to the galley, he looked across at James.

"Typical of the lowering of standards."

"Yes, Peter, there was a time when airlines only employed girls from decent families."

They both knew what Tommy James meant.

Gradually the Boeing Dreamliner climbed over Europe as it burned off fuel.

The Boeing 787 landed on time at O R Tambo airport. As Upper-Class passengers, Holmes and James disembarked ahead of the masses in economy. Ignoring the Asian flight attendant's cheery goodbye, they entered the air bridge and briskly made their way to passport control.

The black officer on duty registered the alert that Holmes' passport caused. As the leader of a racist organisation, he was a 'subject of interest' for the South African security service. Holmes might well suspect that this was the case – but the officer kept a straight face to avoid giving any hint of his distaste for the man's politics.

"Are you here on business or pleasure?"

"Business," Holmes replied.

"How long are you staying?"

"One week."

"And, where are you staying?"

"With friends near Phalaborwa. The address is on the form," he said trying to keep a sneer out of his tone; *'couldn't the idiot see that for himself?'*

"Thank you, Sir. Enjoy your stay."

Holmes took back his passport, passed through the gap between booths then waited for James to join him.

Their luggage dropped onto the carousel not long after they arrived in the baggage hall and they wheeled the cases through customs.

"Would you mind coming over here, please sir?" invited one of the Customs Officers. Another officer asked James to join him at the next table.

"Did you pack your cases yourself?"

"Yes," Holmes replied wearily.

"And are you familiar with this list of prohibited items?" the officer asked, offering a printed sheet.

"Yes, and I don't have any of the items on the list."

"Would you mind opening the case for me please?"

Holmes sighed. There was no doubt in his mind that he had been singled out because of his political views. If this happened at every border, it would be a tedious trip.

The Customs Officer bent over and rummaged through the case. Then stood up.

"Thank you, sir have a good day."

Holmes shook his head as he relocked the case. James had also been allowed to proceed and they walked out of the exit.

"Bastards," James exclaimed quietly.

"Quite," agreed Holmes.

At the exit, they looked around and saw Arnou Bekker, their host, waiting for them. As Holmes reached him, he held out his hand for the other to take.

"Good to see you Arnou."

"You too, Peter." Bekker turned to the youth standing next to him. "This is my lad, Hendrick."

"Good to meet you, Hendrick," said Holmes, taking in the young man's appearance. He was dressed, like his father, in khaki trousers cinched at the waist by a sturdy belt through loops and a matching short-sleeved military-styled shirt with breast pockets and epaulettes and they both wore polished brown shoes and carried wide-brimmed campaign hats.

"Pleased to meet you too, Meneer."

"Hendrick, take Mr Holmes' case." He then turned back to his guest.

"So, how was your flight?"

"Fine,"

"Good, good, the Landcruiser's in the car park. It's about a six-hour drive so we should be at the lodge by about seven. I imagine you'll want to rest this evening after your long journey – so the others won't be joining us until tomorrow."

'Landcruiser? A Jap vehicle? There was a time when the only vehicle of choice in the bush was a British Landrover,' pondered Holmes. *'But, then, the Boers didn't have much cause to love the British. Bekker and his crowd wouldn't be talking to him if it wasn't for a shared enemy.'*

It was easy for Holmes to imagine Bekker senior as one of Jan Smuts' commandos riding against the redcoats – his deep-set eyes, wind-blown face, stereotypical full beard and stocky build could have stepped out of a hundred photographs of the era. His son was slimmer and his facial hair little more than fluff so far – but the likeness was there.

The first half of the journey, heading east from the airport, was through flat farmland with occasional undulations. It then turned northerly and hills started to crowd in each side of the route and on the distant horizon ahead of them and, instead of arrow-straight carriageways as far as they could see, the road twisted and turned. As they left Lydenburg behind them, signs to both sides of the road pointed to private game reserves and the Kruger National Park was only twenty-five miles to the east.

A few miles short of Phalaborwa, Bekker turned off the main road onto a track.

"Nearly there," he announced as the Landcruiser bumped over the uneven surface. Then, as they rounded a bend, the buildings revealed themselves. The main reception was a single-storey traditional Cape Dutch style with white walls and thatched roof over open rafters that allowed the hot air of the day to rise and keep the accommodation cool.

Bekker parked under a portico offering shade during the day but now lit up to welcome the visitors.

Holmes opened the door and stepped out then stretched to ease his aching muscles.

"Boy, take the cases to their rooms. Jump to it," commanded Bekker. The black servant did as he was ordered, making no sign of any resentment he felt; he was aware of Bekker's politics which is why his real employers in the South African Police were concerned about possible white supremacist terrorist attacks, particularly in view of planned attacks on shopping malls in 2019.

Bekker then turned to Holmes and James, "Come, let's have a beer to cut the dust out of our throats – then we can have a shower before dinner. How does that sound? Hendrick, do the honours."

"Sounds good to me," replied Holmes and James in unison.

The next day, they were joined by six other members of Bekker's group to discuss how networks such as theirs could work together to further mutual aims. Neither side had much practical support to offer and if either thought the other would help finance their work, they were to be disappointed. They did, however, amongst the hyperbole, exchange some useful ideas for attracting members and generating income from them.

As the sun set at the end of the day, Bekker took on the role of braai master – building the fire to cook meat that had been marinating for twenty-four hours.

"Have you ever tasted Wildebeest or Warthog?" the host asked Action for England's leaders.

Both shook their heads.

"No, never," said Holmes.

"Nor me," added James.

"Well, you're in for a treat, especially on a braii. Forget your barbecues, this is a whole new level," Bekker told them. "Takes a while before the braai is ready to start cooking, so help yourself to a glass of wine or a beer. Tomorrow, we'll go out in the bush – give you a chance to shoot some game. Can't promise you one of the big five, but there'll certainly be some Springbok. Have you shot before?"

"No, never," admitted Holmes. "Not much opportunity in London – well, not without attracting unwanted attention."

"I guess not, well, man, you'll have the chance tomorrow."

Chapter 39. Ali: Confirmation

Khalid Ali switched on his computer as soon as he arrived at his desk, even before he made a cup of coffee. Opening his e-mails, he scanned the list.

"Yes!" he exclaimed.

He picked up his phone, then put it back on the cradle and strode to Colonel Malik's office. He knocked on the door then entered. He came to attention and saluted his superior.

"We've had confirmation that Holmes and James were on Virgin flight VS 449 to Johannesburg, sir. They are due to land at 11.30 local – that's 13.30 our time."

Malik looked up from the papers on his desk and nodded his head.

"Excellent so they are proceeding according to the itinerary we have?"

"Yes, sir."

"Fine. Now we know the trip is going ahead, you can proceed with the arrangements. You have authority to contact the engineers in Singapore. Keep me informed."

Malik's eyes dropped to the papers on his desk. Ali stood up, saluted and returned to his own desk.

Ensuring the right engineers were on duty on the day – and getting their cooperation was key. But they were good Muslims.

Chapter 40. Michelle Flies to Sydney

While Holmes and James were on their hunting trip, Michelle was checking in at Bangkok airport for her flight to Sydney. She relaxed in the comfort of business class as the Boeing 777 made its overnight voyage south. While it climbed over the South China Sea, she enjoyed the meal served by the Thai Airlines' cabin attendants. As it left Borneo astern, she reclined her seat and pulled the duvet over her. She was conscious that this trip was making a serious dent in the funds that the original Michelle had in her UK bank account – but she was glad she'd booked the more luxurious options for overnight flights.

She was fast asleep, totally oblivious of the moment that the aircraft entered Australian airspace near Darwin. At that point, there were still three hours flying ahead of them. Her breathing was deep with an occasional murmur – contrasting with a portly, ruddy-faced individual two pods away whose snoring was disturbing one of his other neighbours. One of the cabin attendants discreetly offered the victim a pair of earplugs to reduce the noise.

By the time she awoke, feeling refreshed, flight TG475 was ninety minutes from landing. She quickly visited the toilet to change her underwear and wash ready for the cabin crew to serve breakfast.

Once the flight had landed, Michelle made her way through passport control, baggage collection and customs to make her connection to Ayers Rock. As she stood waiting in line, she wondered if she should have allowed an overnight stay in Sydney and travelled on the following day but, in the end, she managed to check in for her next flight with ten minutes to spare.

The next leg of her journey took her back over the red centre of Australia. She had hoped to include a visit to Alice Springs; a desire inspired by reading Neville Shute's 'A Town Like Alice' and watching the film starring Virginia McKenna. Sadly, she'd been unable to coordinate the flights. Michelle was relieved when the plane landed at Ayers Rock and she was able to disembark – only to be hit, once again, by a wave of hot air after being cocooned in air conditioning for the last twenty-four hours. At least this was dry heat rather than the stifling humidity of Bangkok.

It didn't take long for her case to appear on the carousel and she was soon whisked to the hotel on the edge of Ayers Rock resort. The hotel was, unsurprisingly, the most expensive on her entire journey – although the accommodation was not as luxurious as the one in Pattaya. She mused that the side excursion to Ayers Rock had added more than a thousand pounds to the cost of the trip. But you could hardly visit Australia without having a look at Uluru – could you?

Having dilated, showered and changed, she walked back through the grounds of the hotel and the reception to catch the courtesy bus to the centre of the resort where, she'd been told, there were several restaurants that offered a range of meals at a fraction of the hotel's restaurant.

On the edge of the central square, she found a noodle bar called Ayers Wok – which amused her so she decided to eat there despite of the opportunity to have something other than Asian cuisine for the first time in a month.

The following day, Michelle took the tour bus to Uluru. Climbing the rock had been discouraged for several years and eventually banned in 2017 but visitors could still get close to the base and even walk around it. The bus tour didn't allow time to complete the ten-kilometre trek but they spent an hour walking into one of the canyons at the foot of the three hundred-and-fifty-metre-high monolith and take in the visitor centre where they could learn about the Anangu people's culture. The coach then moved on to the viewing area where they were served refreshments while the sun began to set. Most of the passengers had taken out their cameras and found positions next to a wire fence at the edge of the coach park ready to watch the rock change colour as the sun dropped to the horizon. In the scrub, at their feet, tiny mice scuttled around picking up scraps of the picnics provided for the tour passengers.

Back at the hotel, Michelle wandered through the grounds, past the small swimming pool, now deserted, to her room. An hour or so later, she returned to the main building and decided to try out the restaurant rather than go back to the resort centre. After dinner, she moved into the bar, ordered another glass of wine and scanned the other guests. Most seemed to be middle-aged or older; perhaps younger people were more interested in beach holidays rather than culture – or, more likely, didn't think it represented good value.

Her flight to Cairns the next day wasn't until the afternoon – so she was able to enjoy a leisurely breakfast and pack her cases before the courtesy bus to the airport.

The departure lounge had a small refreshment counter offering mainly sandwiches and hot and cold drinks. Michelle ordered a cola and a tuna mayonnaise sandwich which she ate while waiting for her flight to board. As she couldn't see a Qantas aircraft on the apron, she assumed it was still on its way from Cairns. A Jetstar was preparing to leave – its passengers had just been called to the gate and the first ones were soon walking out of the door and along the marked route to climb the stairs to board the aircraft. There were also a few small aircraft outside the terminal –

including some high-wing single-engine aircraft that looked like they held four people and some brightly coloured helicopters.

As the queue for the Jetstar dwindled, Michelle saw a twin-engine jet with a red tail bearing a kangaroo design landing on the runway. A few minutes later, it pulled up next to the Jetstar and was soon surrounded by the vehicles needed to refuel, replenish its supplies, empty the toilets, collect the baggage and position the stairs for the passengers to disembark.

Chapter 41. A4E Arrive Sydney

olmes and James were both tired by the time their flight from Johannesburg touched down in Sydney. In spite of the extra legroom in business class, neither had been able to sleep well. They'd left the Bekker's game lodge early the previous morning and had been travelling for more than twenty-one hours – and it was likely to be another two to three hours before they reached their hotel rooms.

Once again, their passports raised alerts as they passed through immigration. Not that this held them up very much this time. Their cases hadn't arrived when they reached the baggage hall.

"I need the toilet," Holmes told James.

"OK, if you go first, I'll watch out for our cases."

The conveyor operated in fits and starts with just a few bags being deposited each time and their luggage still hadn't arrived when Holmes returned.

"Right, Tommy, you go and sort yourself out," Holmes instructed his deputy.

Tommy James knew better than to take his time – if the cases arrived before he returned, Holmes would be irritable and it would show. In the end, it didn't matter. Their bags were amongst the last to drop onto the conveyor.

They then made their way to the green channel – only to be stopped by customs.

Holmes shut his eyes and tightened his lips.

"Not again," he said under his breath to James. "This is getting fucking stupid and if I don't have a smoke soon, I'm going to snap."

As in South Africa, they subjected their cases to scrutiny and confirmed that they had nothing on the banned items list. And, as in South Africa, they were allowed to proceed when no prohibited items were found.

Finally, they left the terminal building and found a smoking area where they were able to light up and draw craved nicotine into their system.

"Come on, let's find a cab and get to the hotel," said Holmes.

Fortunately, the queue for cabs wasn't long, the drive to the hotel quite short and the registration process painless.

"I need a drink, arrange for the cases to be taken up to our rooms," Holmes told James. "I'll go and get them in at the bar."

"Fine. Make mine a long one."

Holmes marched across the foyer into the adjacent bar.

"What can I get you, Sir?" asked the barman.

Holmes thought for a moment. He hadn't been out in the sun long while having a smoke and waiting for a taxi – but it was mid-summer and hot. He needed something to quench his thirst and a brandy wouldn't do that.

"Give me two lagers," he told him.

"Bottles, schooners or pints?"

Seeing Holmes hesitate, the barman explained.

"A schooner of draft is 425 millilitres – more than a bottle but less than a pint."

"Schooners then."

"Just arrived in Oz, have you?" asked the barman.

"Why do you ask?"

"Just making conversation mate. You seemed a bit uncertain about drinks here."

Holmes looked at him as he picked up one of the glasses of lager and took a sip. With his short blond hair and blue eyes, the barman could have been a poster model for the Third Reich's Ayrian race. Of course, his hair could have been bleached by the sun – he was well-tanned.

As he assessed him, James joined Holmes.

"Is that mine?" he asked – pointing to the second glass which was gathering condensation.

"It is."

James wiped his finger through the dew then lifted it to his lips and drained half the glass in one swallow.

He breathed out loudly as he sat the glass back on the counter.

"I needed that. The cases are being taken to the rooms and I checked on the room we've got booked for the meetings. Everything's sorted."

"Excellent. Right, once I've finished this drink, I'm going to have a shower then a nap. Dinner at eight thirty suit you?"

James knew the question was hypothetical. If Holmes suggested eight thirty – then eight thirty it was.

Following three days of meetings which followed a similar pattern to that in South Africa, Holmes and James spent the Christmas holiday at a cattle station owned by the leader of one of the groups.

On Christmas morning, they attended a church service with their hosts – ironically celebrating the birth of an olive-skinned infant while their aims were to cleanse their countries of similar individuals.

Chapter 42. Ali in Dubai

So, it *IS* possible to make it appear that there is a fault with one of the engines?" Khalid Ali asked.

"Certainly. If you have engineers you can trust to insert a device during the aircraft's final stop before the flight you want diverting," the technician replied.

"And you can produce the device we need?"

"Indeed. But I don't have access to aircraft in service – only those that are in for servicing or repairs."

"That's not the problem, the flight won't be leaving from here. We can arrange for the device to be fitted by the ground crew."

"You do realise that the engine monitoring system will transmit the fault indication to the manufacturer?"

"That's what we want."

"Then it can be done."

Chapter 43. Michelle: Cairns

Sixteen hundred miles north of Holmes and James, Michelle checked into a hotel near the seafront. She'd arranged to tick off three more items from her bucket list while in Cairns: a ride on the Kurada scenic railway; sailing on the Great Barrier Reef and diving on the reef.

The six week wait after surgery before swimming again expired on Boxing Day so she'd booked two days diving for 26th and 27th December. Not having evidence of diving in the last year, she did, however, need to carry out a pool check-dive before going out on the boat and had arranged that for Christmas Eve. She was breaking her surgeon's guidance but didn't think two days would matter.

After a day just wandering around Cairns and watching the boats at the marina, Michelle got up early on Friday and made her way to the railway station to join one of the Gold Class carriages and took her seat. The carriage quickly filled up as the time for departure approached. An elderly couple, smiled as they took the seats opposite her.

"Good morning, my dear, what a glorious morning for our trip," the woman remarked. "I'm Joyce, by the way, and this is my husband, Raymond. Have you done this trip before?"

"No, this is my first visit to Australia."

"Well, I think we're in for a treat, the scenery is supposed to be spectacular. Are you also doing the cableway ride?"

"Yes, I am. Are you?"

"No, Raymond doesn't like heights as he discovered when we did Table Mountain in South Africa."

Raymond pouted his lips and harumphed – Michelle could see, however, that there was a twinkle in his eye and realised that Joyce was just teasing him and he was taking it in good humour.

"This trip is to celebrate our golden wedding anniversary – it should have been eighteen months ago but Covid got in the way."

'Golden wedding. Married for fifty years. She and Deborah had managed just twelve years.' Michelle thought. *'Would she find anyone else in the future? It seemed unlikely. Well, that might be the price she'd pay for the step she'd taken.'*

As predicted, the trip was spectacular and Michelle had dozens of photographs to sort through when she got back to her hotel.

The next morning, she packed her bikini and a towel in a beach bag and caught a cab to the dive company's office.

A tall, tanned blonde wearing cut-off shorts and loose T-shirt over a bikini top, her long hair in a ponytail welcomed her.

"Hi, Michelle, I'm Sharon, I'll be doing your check dive and leading your group on the boat. I gather you've dived before, is that right?"

"Just a few on holiday. I haven't done a full course. And, it's been a while; what with Covid."

"OK. Well, let's see what you remember."

Sharon picked a Buoyancy Control Device, set of regulators and a tank.

"Do you remember how to rig the tank and BCD?"

"Might be best if you run through it for me."

Once they'd set up the jacket and tank and Sharon had run through the checks she'd need to make, Michelle changed into her bikini and pulled on a shorty wetsuit before joining Sharon again at the side of the training pool where she chose a pair of fins a mask and snorkel. Sharon then helped her into the buoyancy jacket with the heavy tank strapped to it.

In the water, they ran through some basic drills then swimming along the bottom – getting used to the feel of the kit and practising her breathing. After fifteen minutes or so, she felt quite relaxed and in control.

Back on the side of the pool, Sharon declared herself satisfied that Michelle was competent to undertake dives to fifteen metres.

"It's a pity you're not in Cairns for a week – we could have got you qualified," Sharon told her.

"Maybe another time."

When she woke the next morning, Michelle realised it was Christmas Day. The second since becoming Michelle and the second without her family. Those memories now seemed to belong to a different person – which was quite accurate; she was very different to the individual who had joined the train fourteen months earlier. Her Christmas would also be very different to any previous ones. Instead of the possibility of snow on the ground and turkey and all the trimmings around a dining table – she was joining a barbecue on the beach under the midsummer sun. Back in the UK, the Queen's message that had been part of every Christmas she'd ever known – even if she hadn't watched them – would be replaced by one by King Charles.

As soon as Michelle joined the group on the beach for the dive centre's barbecue, Sharon offered her a can of lager and introduced her to other members of staff and other customers who were on the dive trip with her.

The afternoon and evening were spent eating and drinking, much as it would have been in the UK. The setting, however, was very different. As the sun dipped below the horizon, the music was turned up and everyone started dancing around a large bonfire. At first, it was a general mêlée but, as the evening went on, the dancers tended to pair off. A few, including Michelle, were still keeping their own space but Daniel, one of the male instructors, was frequently turning towards her and matching her moves.

"I need a drink," she told him as the DJ merged one tune into another.

"Good idea," Daniel agreed, walking with her to the bar where he picked up a can, opened it and handed it to her before opening one for himself.

"Cheers," he said tapping his can against hers.

"Shall we sit over there?" he asked pointing to a blanket spread out on the sand. Michelle was anxious not to lead him on – still conscious of her experience with Cliff in Pattaya and he was a lot younger than her – but turning down his suggestion seemed unreasonable. As she sat down, she positioned herself to face Daniel; close enough to chat but not to invite him to reach for her.

"So, Michelle, where in the UK are you from?" he asked.

"I live in Manchester – well, Salford."

"That's not where you were born though from your accent."

Michelle had to think quickly to remember where the original Michelle had been born.

"No, I moved there for work. I was born in Berkshire. What about you? Where are you from?"

"Witney in Oxfordshire."

"So, are you on holiday?"

"I'm taking a gap year travelling around. I finished veterinary training in the summer. Couldn't be here and not dive the reef. Have you dived before?"

"I worked in Dubai for a while – so did a few dives there and on holidays. Hopefully, this will have a lot more to see. How about you?"

"I've done a few – mainly in the Red Sea. Some interesting trips; I particularly like the Thistlegorm."

"I've heard of that – wasn't it a supply ship from the war with lots of vehicles and other things on board."

"That's the one. Nothing like that here – but plenty of colourful corals and fish."

"Well, to be honest, I'd far rather see those than a scrapyard," Michelle remarked with a smile.

"I guess it is more of a blokey thing, looking at all the weapons and fighting machines."

"Probably," agreed Michelle – pleased that she couldn't be displaying any male traits for him to pick up on. She felt relaxed in his company and he was attractive and was flattered by his attention. She wondered if he would make any moves on her – and how she'd react if he did. A kiss might be nice. She wouldn't even mind a cuddle. The problem was that he'd probably want more. Heck, she'd probably want more. She did want more – but it was still too soon after surgery. Another month and it would be OK – but not yet.

The fire was dying down as she drained her can of lager.

"I'm going to call it a night, I want to be fit for tomorrow," she announced as she stood up.

"I'll see you back to your hotel," Daniel told her.

"There's no need, I can manage,"

"I've got to go that way in any case."

Michelle couldn't see any way of avoiding his company without being rude but when he offered her his hand to help her up, she pretended not to notice and kept a couple of feet away from him as they walked along the promenade.

"Right, this is me," she said as they reached the entrance to her hotel. "Thanks for the company," she added holding out a hand for him to shake. She could see the disappointment in his eyes as he took it.

"See you in the morning, Daniel."

"Yeah, g'night Michelle," he replied, turning away with his head down.

After breakfast the next morning, she put a t-shirt and shorts on over her bikini and packed a change of underwear and a towel in her bag. She dropped her keys at reception and waited at the kerb for the dive centre's minibus to pick her up.

She was the last of the guests to be collected and it was only a ten-minute drive to the marina where the dive boat was moored against one of the pontoons. Michelle collected the kit she'd used for her pool refresher from the store and added a stinger suit to protect her from Box Jellyfish; the crew had already loaded the air tanks.

On the way to the reef, the crew briefed the divers on what to expect. They were then allocated 'buddies' that they would dive with.

"Make sure you stay with your buddy throughout the dive," warned Sharon, the leader of Michelle's group. "I'll be leading the way – so watch for my signals too. Keep an eye on your air levels and let me know if you're running low. We'll be staying quite shallow most of the time around ten to twelve metres so it shouldn't be a problem. We'll carry out a decompression stop on the way back up – resting for three minutes at around five metres. Any questions?"

At the dive site, the buddies checked each other's kit. They all then waddled in their cumbersome fins to the edge of the dive platform and stepped off with a large stride, they sank under the water before the air in their BCDs brought them back to the surface. Each of them gave the 'OK' signal to Sharon as she checked they were happy. Satisfied everyone was fine, she gave her group the thumbs down signal indicating that they should release some of the air from their BCDs and start to descend.

The seven divers gradually sank down, Sharon watching each one of her charges and checking they were still comfortable – with the 'are you OK?' signal. As they'd been briefed, the others returned her signal. Sharon then led them along just above the colourful coral as fish of all hues and shapes and sizes darted around them.

Michelle's eyes flicked from one side to the other as different targets caught her attention. There were orange and white Clown Fish hiding amongst the tentacles of the anemones and bright Blue Tang Surgeonfish with their yellow tails – Nemo and Dory the stars of Finding Nemo; Angelfish with their vertical stripes and Butterflyfish; spotted Leopard Wrasse a few centimetres long and Maori Wrasse, their bigger cousins, which could reach more than two metres long. Spiny Lionfish hid in crevasses while turtles used their flippers in a kind of breaststroke as they swam away from the human invaders.

Back on board, the more advanced divers in Daniel's group, who had ventured deeper than Michelle's, reported having seen some White Tipped Reef Sharks and some rays.

As lunch was served, the boat moved to another reef for the afternoon's dives. Michelle lost track of the different fish – there were too many species to remember.

Chapter 44. A4E: Fly to New Zealand

While Michelle enjoyed a second day's diving, Holmes and James were resuming their hectic schedule after their Christmas break – spending more time in airports and flying than in their meetings with other groups in Melbourne, Adelaide and Brisbane before crossing the Tasman Sea to New Zealand. At least they'd then have two nights in the same hotel in Wellington before resuming their frenetic tour with their final discussions with a group in Auckland.

Then it would be back to Sydney for a final night's rest before the long trip back to the UK.

Chapter 45. Michelle: Sailing in Cairns

I t was Michelle's last day in Cairns. Tomorrow, she'd be flying back to Sydney for the New Year's celebrations. She would have loved another day underwater, 'blowing bubbles' as they called it, but that wasn't allowed. You had to leave twenty-four hours between diving and flying. Instead, she'd booked a sailing trip around the reefs on the 'Island Maid'.

As the yacht left the harbour, one of the crew took hold of a rope near where she was sitting, wrapped it a couple of times around a winch and started to wind it in.

"Would you like me to tail that for you?" she'd asked, knowing that it helped to keep tension on the rope as the winch was turned.

"Have you done much sailing before?" he asked as he coiled the rope after hauling in the sail.

"A bit," she confirmed.

"I suspect rather more than a bit, after your offer," he suggested.

"A friend had a yacht on the Hamble back in the UK and I used to sail with him. We did a few cross-channel races."

"Right! Well, let us know if you want to take a turn on the helm later."

"I will, that would be great."

The yacht was heeling over slightly as it cut through the water, the bow occasionally burying itself in the waves, throwing spray back along the deck. Overhead gulls screeched and wheeled in the clear blue sky. The sun was climbing higher and already beating down. Thankfully, the two main sails provided plenty of shade for the twenty-odd passengers.

Michelle stood up and made her way closer to the front of the boat. She was pleased to note that she hadn't lost her sea legs since she was last on a yacht. Her friend's boat, or rather Jeff's friend's boat had been twelve metres long with a single mast. This was at least twice as long with two masts.

As she sat on the cabin roof forward of the foremast, she scanned the sea ahead. Suddenly about a kilometre ahead of them and slightly off the starboard bow, a giant shape emerged from the water. It seemed to stand on the surface, its fins down by its side before falling back with a huge splash – the tail then emerging before it, too, disappeared below the waves.

"Whale," one of the crew called out pointing at the place where it had disappeared below the surface. "Just breached off the starboard bow. Keep your eyes peeled everyone it may come up again – or there may be others."

Michelle had been so mesmerised by the sight of the monster that she hadn't taken out her camera to photograph it. Now she took it out of her bag and switched it on in case the whale reappeared and wasn't disappointed. It seemed to relish in performing for the boat's passengers, giving them opportunities for photographs that would impress their friends when they related their experiences.

After a stop at the white sandy beach of one of the islands, where the passengers could explore the clear waters, the crew weighed anchor and turned Island Maid back towards Cairns. Some of the guests had taken advantage of the break to dive, others, including Michelle, had snorkelled instead – or simply splashed around.

As the yacht made its way home, the crew served a buffet from which Michelle filled a plate then found a space on the cabin roof to sit and eat. As Jeff, she'd rarely watched what she ate, these days she was conscious of her figure and anxious to stay as slim as possible – another of the prices she'd paid for her transition.

"Can I take that plate if you've finished?" asked one of the crew.

"Have you enjoyed the trip?" she added as Michelle handed it to her.

"It's been magic. Seeing the whales was incredible."

"They certainly are, I'm fortunate having this as my 'office'."

While she moved on to collect used crockery from other passengers, Michelle stood up and walked to the wheelhouse. She stood at the open door.

"Hi. Kyle said it might be possible to have a go at helming," she said to the tall blonde woman at the wheel. *'Were all of the women in the dive centres and on the boats tall blondes,'* she wondered.

"Hi, yes, he said someone might be interested. You've done some sailing in the UK I gather."

"Yes, not on anything this big, mainly on a Sunfast 37 around the Solent and Channel and a couple of flotillas in the Med."

"Fine, well, the Maid might take a little longer to respond but it's basically the same," she remarked, standing to one side to let Michelle take the wheel.

"We're heading just to port of that headland," she said pointing ahead.

As the afternoon Virgin Airways Boeing 737 raced down the runway then climbed away from Cairns, Michelle looked out at the islands and reefs of the Great Barrier Reef. Would she see it again? There was no reason why she shouldn't make a return visit. Her job with Cavanagh System Solutions seemed to be secure. She had a very pleasant apartment in Salford Quays, money in the bank and there'd been no complications following her surgery. Two guys had apparently found her attractive enough to chat her up – and the thought of taking it further with a man excited her.

She thought back over the last few days – the diving had been fabulous; so much to see. She planned to do a full course and qualifying so she could dive even deeper. The sailing had also been brilliant – maybe next time she came she'd combine sailing round the Whitsunday Islands with some diving. As far as she could see, there was no limit to what she could do.

Now she was looking forward to a few days in Sydney including the New Year's Eve firework display – reckoned to be one of the most spectacular displays in the world. When she'd been planning her trip, she'd looked up the area where the Australian, Glen, had been born and spent most of his childhood. It was close to another place she'd seen on television – Bathurst, famous for car racing around Mount Panorama.

She'd decided to visit Glen's home town to pay homage to his history as his death had given her the chance to live as Michelle. Afterwards, she'd drive around the Bathurst raceway. The trip there and back would take her through the Blue Mountains – making a fitting end to her odyssey.

Chapter 46. Ali: Singapore

Khalid Ali flew into Singapore on New Year's Day with Sami Harib, the technician from Dubai. The next morning, they met with the engineers who would be servicing the aircraft carrying Homes and James back to the UK. Harib switched on his laptop and opened a file showing the servicing diagram for the huge Airbus 380 engines.

"You will need to remove this panel here," he told them, pointing to the relevant item on the screen. "Remove the insulating strip to activate the battery, then clip the device around this cable and refit the panel. That's all."

"Seems straightforward, I assume it generates a signal in the wiring?" remarked Abdul Ghonim.

"Yes, that signal will indicate a fault in the engine," replied Harib.

"How is it triggered? Presumably a timer is unreliable as the flight could be delayed," asked Ibrahim Aziz.

"You don't need to know how it works, you just need to do as you are asked," Ali told him.

"OK, I was just being curious. It will be done as you ask," conceded Aziz.

"The target flight should be Thursday night. If that changes, I will let you know. I will confirm on the day in any case, Inshallah."

"So long as it isn't delayed by more than two days. Our rota might change after that."

"Understood. Any other questions? Aziz? Ghonim? No? Maʿ al-salāmah."

"Fī amān Allāh," recited Aziz and Ghonim as they stood and left.

Chapter 47. A4E: Back to Sydney

ow many meetings have we had in the last three weeks? Twelve? The question is, were they worthwhile?" Homes said to James, his deputy, as the Qantas Boeing carried them across the Tasman Sea from Wellington to Sydney.

"Well, we've picked up some ideas for attracting members and getting allies elected to local councils. We just about covered our travel costs from the development fund and speakers' fees. If nothing else, we avoided that miserable lead-up to Christmas in London."

"That's certainly true. Well, one more night in a hotel – then the flight back to England. Pity we didn't have time to visit Raffles Hotel – it was always a bastion of the Englishmen who built the place," Holmes remarked.

"We could have broken the journey and stayed there for one night," James replied.

"Not at over a thousand pounds a night each, unfortunately, Tommy."

"Probably not the same as it was anyway, Peter. Overrun by foreign tourists these days I bet. Can't say I'm looking forward to twenty-four hours from Sydney to London."

"Nor am I, but the only alternative was to transit through Dubai or Abu Dhabi. Or break the journey in Singapore – even if not at Raffles."

"I know. At least we'll be able to stretch out in business class. Let's hope we sleep better than we did between Jo'burg and Sydney."

Chapter 48. Michelle: Heads Home

ichelle checked out of her hotel and caught the shuttle bus to the airport. Her flight was due to leave just after five pm. There was a stop-over in Singapore before it flew on, overnight, to London. She'd then have the final leg to Manchester. She reflected that she could have saved half a day by flying via Dubai – but there was a little matter of the money in the account in Liechtenstein and the possibility that it related to something the original Michelle had done in the Emirate.

Chapter 49. A4E: Check In

Holmes and James joined the business class baggage drop queue for the flight behind Michelle. Had Tommy James been aware of her transgender history, he'd have regarded her with disgust – but all he saw was an attractive white female. If she was on the same flight, perhaps there'd be an opportunity to chat her up. That might help pass the time.

As Michelle walked towards the security gates, the two A4E leaders took her place in front of the desk, hoisted their cases onto the scales and handed over their papers.

"Did you pack the bags yourself?" the agent asked in a tone that made it obvious they were as tired of asking the question as passengers were of answering.

Having received the appropriate responses, they attached tags to the cases and pressed the button for the conveyor belt to carry them out of sight.

Chapter 50. Waiting to Board

Having cleared security, Michelle wandered through duty-free, spending time looking at some jewellery and buying a bottle of her favourite Manifesto perfume. Seeing she still had an hour before her flight was due to board, she went into the business lounge and took advantage of the refreshments on offer.

Sipping her coffee, she noticed two men sprawled on sofas the other side of the room, legs splayed out, occupying as much space as possible. Next to them were carrier bags from duty-free containing bottles of Scotch according to the ends of the boxes she could see. Each man held a glass of amber liquid that Michelle assumed to be whisky – no doubt from the complimentary bar, not their own purchases.

As she glanced at them, Holmes downed the remainder of his drink and held his glass towards James.

"Get me a refill, old boy – and grab some more of those pastries while you're at it."

The two looked vaguely familiar but Michelle couldn't place them at first. Then it clicked and she remembered seeing Peter Holmes, the leader of Action for England, on the news after the train bombing – blaming Islamic terrorists. His extreme right-wing views were totally at odds with her own.

As James returned to his seat with the replenished glasses of whisky and a plate of pastries, he caught sight of Michelle as she glanced at him and realised it was the woman who'd been in front of him in at baggage drop. Mistaking her look as suggesting interest, he smiled at her.

Michelle was horrified to have been caught observing him – and the way he'd returned her look. Did he really think she'd be interested in him? In your dreams, mister.

She dropped her eyes to her iPad and opened the book she'd downloaded for the flight.

James was used to being dismissed by women; salving his esteem by shrugging his shoulders and regarding them as 'stuck up bitches' or 'dykes'.

When the information screen showed their flight was boarding, Holmes and James stood up and briskly headed to the gate. Michelle took her time, seeing little point in waiting in the queue. It wasn't as though they needed to fight for space in the overhead lockers for their carry-on bags like those in economy. She just hoped she wouldn't be seated close to the A4E pair.

Despite her efforts to leave space between them and her, they were only a few places ahead of her when they were called forward for boarding. She was relieved to see them turn left on entering the upper deck of the aircraft while her seat was next to a window behind the wing.

Khalid Ali had also been observing Holmes and James when they boarded the aircraft. He'd reserved a window seat that allowed him to see the number three engine the ground crew in Singapore would be tampering with. He would also be able to observe Holmes and James and be close to them when they landed.

Soon after five o'clock, the massive aircraft was pushed back from the gate and taxied to the runway. Holmes, James and Ali in the forward cabin hardly heard any sound from the huge turbofans; further back, Michelle heard the engines whine then screech as the turbines spooled up to take-off power and thrust the behemoth of the skies down the two-and-a-half-mile runway. After covering three-quarters of the length, the forward undercarriage left the asphalt and the Airbus started its long climb to cruising altitude.

Michelle looked down at the rapidly retreating ground – watching as it became a toy landscape. The coastal area gave way to the Blue Mountains, which she'd driven through a couple of days ago. She tried to identify Bathurst but it was probably on the other side of the aircraft. Below her, she could see pillars of smoke from forest fires – fed, no doubt, by the oily eucalyptus trees. This seemed to be a perennial problem for New South Wales as the summers got hotter.

Gradually, the rich vegetation was left behind and the aircraft crept over the outback and the red interior. After miles of nothing, Michelle made out a town that could only be Alice Springs. It had been one of the places she'd have liked to visit – but it hadn't been possible to fit it into her schedule. Perhaps next time.

At the front of the aircraft, Holmes and James weren't interested in the country passing seven miles below them. As soon as they could, they demanded glasses of whisky. By the time they were over Alice Springs, they were on their third miniature bottles.

Khalid Ali was concerned about the amount of alcohol Holmes and James had drunk. Not that he cared about the state of their liver or any religious reservations, he was worried that if they drank too much, there was the risk of them being taken off the flight in Singapore and that would destroy months of careful planning. Fortunately, the cabin staff had started to serve dinner which might help to absorb some of the Scotch.

Ali needn't have worried, as the detritus from dinner was cleared away, Holmes and James ordered a brandy each – then reclined their seats and closed their eyes.

Their snores caused other passengers in the cabin to raise their eyebrows and shake their heads at the pair of uncouth and inconsiderate travellers and hope fervently that they would be leaving the aircraft in Singapore – as unlikely as that seemed.

They were woken by one of the cabin crew as the aircraft approached Singapore.

"Could you return your seats to the upright position please gentlemen and fasten your seat belts?" he asked.

"I need the toilet first," Holmes told him.

"Me too," added James.

"Please be quick then, we are about to land," the attendant told them.

Ali could hear the conversation and smiled to himself. He knew the crew had anticipated the need for the toilet and had allowed for it when waking them.

Chapter 51. Changi Airport, Singapore

As the aircraft undercarriage kissed the runway at Changi Airport, Ali sent a message to Ghonim and Aziz to confirm that they should proceed with their plan. The stop-over in Singapore was less than two hours – demanding a choreographed ballet of services pulling up to the aircraft to refuel, dispose of waste, and replenish other supplies. Some passengers disembarked to stretch their legs while others stayed in their seats with cleaners working around them. The open doors allowed the hot humid evening air to enter the previously cocooned fuselage, carrying with it the smells of burned aviation fuel.

Michelle decided to join those passengers taking some exercise before the long leg to Heathrow. There was little time to do more than pass through immigration then make their way back to the gate to reboard – but at least it made a change of scene.

Holmes and James were desperate for a dose of nicotine so left the aircraft to find the smoking area.

Ali wondered whether to remain on board or follow the A4E leaders. As they'd left their carry-on cases and coats, he was confident they would reboard and he stayed in his seat and looked out of the window. Amongst the workers on the tarmac, he could see Ghonim and Aziz approach the number three engine.

As the cabin crew closed the aircraft doors after the last of the returning passengers, Ali's phone bleeped with an incoming message.

"Done," it read.

"Excellent," Ali responded.

A few minutes after midnight, the replenished Airbus lifted back into the air and set course over the Andaman Sea towards the Indian subcontinent.

Michelle reclined her seat as soon as she could and was blissfully unaware as the aircraft continued to climb to cruising altitude over the Bay of Bengal before entering Indian airspace where it continued to cover a mile on the ground below every six and a half seconds.

Holmes demanded a scotch from the flight attendant then, savouring the smooth liquid, closed his eyes. Once he'd finished the nightcap he hoped would help him sleep, he reclined his seat. Tommy James had already dozed off.

Knowing nothing was likely to happen for about six hours, Ali also reclined his seat as the cabin crew dimmed the lights.

In the cockpit, the pilot and first officer monitored the instruments. Everything was as it should be. The engines were running smoothly and the autopilot was keeping the aircraft, with nearly five hundred souls on board, on track.

A few minutes after passing over the point where Afghanistan, Pakistan and Iran meet, the GPS receiver in the device fitted by Ghonim and Aziz registered that it had reached the longitude of fifty-nine degrees East. It woke and induced a signal into the cable it was wrapped around.

In the cockpit, the temperature gauge for the number three engine started to rise. An alarm sounded, attracting the crew's attention.

Chapter 52. Pan, Pan, Pan

The first officer opened the folder containing checklists for various eventualities and called out the steps while the captain confirmed that appropriate actions had been taken.

Underlying their calm exchanges, both felt the rush of adrenalin. It was often said that flying a big jet was 99% boredom and 1% terror. They weren't at the terror stage – the aircraft could fly safely on three engines – but it was sensible to land as soon as possible in case of a second or third engine failure. Dubai was approximately an hour south of their position; the engine manufacturer had a substantial maintenance facility to support a large fleet of 380s based there.

The first officer put out a call on the radio. "Pan-pan, pan-pan, pan-pan. Dubai Control, Dubai Control, Dubai Control. Flight Quebec Foxtrot One. Our position is approximately three-one degrees zero minutes North, five-nine degrees zero minutes East. We have malfunction on engine three. Request diversion to Dubai. Four hundred and seventy-five passengers and crew on board. Over."

Dubai control approved the diversion and the aircraft banked to port as the pilot altered course.

Khalid Ali smiled as he felt the aircraft change direction and noticed the engine nearest the fuselage on his side power down.

Holmes, James and Michelle continued to sleep, blissfully unaware, for the moment, of the new destination.

Having dealt with the initial alarm, the captain briefed the cabin staff to wake the passengers and prepare them for landing in about sixty minutes.

"This is the Captain speaking, we have a possible problem with one of our engines. There's no danger, the aircraft can easily fly on just three engines. However, we always put safety first so we are diverting to Dubai and expect to arrive in about an hour. We apologise for the disruption this will cause. The airline will arrange onward travel. If necessary, we will arrange hotel accommodation for you."

There were various reactions to the news that the aircraft would now land at Dubai.

For some passengers, it was an inconvenience – they had plans, including onward flights, that would now be affected. Others were pleased that they might get to see the Burj Khalifa and would have another country to tick off their bucket list.

Michelle, Holmes and James were amongst those who were not happy with the news.

Holmes and James didn't anticipate any problems, they just didn't want to be in an Arab country amongst the ragheads.

"Fuck, that's the last thing we needed, Peter, Christ, hope they don't connect us with the train," James hissed.

"Keep quiet, you fool. How could they? Unless you've been talking, we're the only ones who know about it."

"I haven't said a word to anyone."

"So how could they possibly have any idea? Just stay calm – you're more likely to cause suspicion if you look nervous. In any case, we don't have anything to hide here."

"So long as they don't make things difficult for us, our views are well known after all."

"So, what can they do to us? We haven't committed any offences in the UAE. Just be polite to them – even if it sticks in the craw. With luck, we'll be out of there before long. Probably won't even have to leave the airport."

"You're right, Peter, I'm worrying about nothing."

Michelle wasn't sure if there would be any difficulties. She didn't think the money in Liechtenstein would be a problem, there hadn't been any sign of the authorities investigating a significant loss.

There was, however, a risk that one of Michelle's former colleagues might recognise her. She'd researched the major characters in 'her' life in the gulf – but there could be dozens of acquaintances who might recognise her. What would she do if someone did say something?

Ali was confident the next stage of his plan was in place.

The only real risk had been that the flight crew wouldn't divert to Dubai when they identified a problem with the engine. They could have ignored the warning or even diverted elsewhere. But Dubai, home of Emirates airline with more than a hundred A380s, the largest fleet of the type, with facilities to match, was the logical destination. As one of Qantas's partner airlines, If they couldn't resolve the problem, no one could.

While the plane flew south, cabin crew checked which passengers had onward flights that could be achieved by switching them to other airlines in Dubai and staff on the ground did their best to accommodate their preferences. Priority was given to members of the airline's frequent flyer programme – which didn't include Michelle or the A4E pair. The latter had been put at the end of the queue by a customer services agent whose cousin had been injured after a clash between A4E and an anti-fascist group he belonged to.

Flight QF1 skirted the Iranian islands near the Strait of Hormuz then remained over the waters of the Persian Gulf until it was time to line up with the runway at Dubai Airport. As it touched down, emergency vehicles swung onto the runway then desperately strived to catch up as it decelerated from a touch-down speed of a hundred and fifty miles an hour. They caught up with it as it slowed to about sixty. They could see no sign of any fire or other damage to the engine and advised that there was no need to carry out an emergency evacuation. The pilot pulled off the runway onto a taxiway where he stopped the aircraft for a closer check. The crews of the fire tenders approached the starboard wing and checked the engine. Happy that there was no danger of fire or other threats, they signalled for the pilot to take the Airbus to a vacant gate at the terminal.

Chapter 53. A4E: Transfer

The cabin staff disembarked passengers who now had onward flights first; leaving Holmes and his deputy to sit in their seats as almost all of the other passengers in the forward cabin made their way into the terminal.

Outside, engineers were approaching the engine that had appeared to be overheating. As Khalid Ali had arranged, they removed the device that had caused the spurious signal then went through the motions of replacing several temperature sensors and appeared to carry out a very thorough visual inspection of the engine.

In the cabin, Khalid Ali approached Holmes and James.

"Mr Holmes, Mr James, my name is Ali," he said. "We have made special arrangements for your transfer. As you may appreciate, your political views are not popular in this part of the world so we thought it best to avoid the need for you to go through the main terminal. We don't want any unpleasantness reflecting on our reputation for hospitality. Please collect any hand baggage and come with me."

The three of them entered the airbridge but, instead of continuing into the terminal, they took stairs down to the ground level where a car was waiting for them. The driver took their hand baggage and put it in the luggage compartment.

"Your other cases will be transferred to your onward flight but we're taking you to a private office while you wait."

Holmes and James shrugged their shoulders at each other and climbed into the back of the Mercedes SUV while Ali joined the driver in the front.

Bemused, rather than suspicious or worried, the A4E men sat back as the driver radioed for permission to proceed airside and switched on his roof-mounted amber hazard lights. There was no sense of urgency as they drove around the perimeter track, stopping at intersections to give way to aircraft.

They eventually drew up outside a hangar bearing the sign Habban Aviation. On the apron outside the office was a small transport plane.

"Please come into the office," Ali invited as they got out of the car. "The driver will bring your bags in."

Ali stood aside as they entered, then followed them into the reception with a comfortable seating area leading off it. A table along one wall carried coffee filter machines.

"Help yourself to refreshments, gentlemen," Ali invited.

Distracted by the offer, Holmes and James didn't notice the driver and another individual entering the office. They took positions either side of the door, standing 'at ease', arms behind them, and watched Ali. At a nod from him, they brought their arms into view – hands holding pistols pointing at the two A4E leaders who were pouring coffees, their backs to the Habbanese Intelligence officers.

"Please put down your cups and turn around with your hands in the air," Ali instructed.

"What the fuck!" James exclaimed when he saw the guns pointing at them.

"You didn't really think scum like you deserved to be treated as honoured guests, did you?" asked Ali. "Mr Holmes, step over to the wall, lean forward and place your hands on it. Now you Mr James."

While his colleagues kept Holmes and James covered, Ali carefully searched the prisoners. Satisfied they didn't have any hidden weapons, he instructed them to strip to their underwear in turn and put on orange jumpsuits he handed them. He then pulled their arms behind them and bound their wrists with heavy-duty cable ties.

"You won't get away with this," Holmes blustered, "The British government will complain to the UAE authorities."

"That won't help you. Your Home Office hasn't been happy with your activities for some time and Foreign Office enquiries might well be protracted."

Ali's two subordinates each took one of the A4E men by the arm and forced them out of the office and across the fifty yards of apron to the transport aircraft. They bundled them into the rear of the cargo space and brusquely pushed them on the floor with their backs to a bulkhead. The officers then sat in seats facing them — still covering them with their weapons.

Ali checked that the cargo was secure as the plane taxied to the runway.

"I know what you're thinking; that we won't dare use the pistols when airborne as piercing the fuselage would decompress the cabin. Sorry to disappoint you – but that wouldn't be catastrophic for this aircraft. We won't be flying higher than five thousand feet so it wouldn't matter; well not to the aircraft – it would be catastrophic for you."

Thirty minutes after taking off from Dubai, the box-shaped Skyvan landed on the short strip at Kilometre Eighteen, the base used by the Americans for Extraordinary Rendition — forced abduction of subjects for interrogation using techniques that would not be allowed in the United States — or other major western powers. It had been used increasingly since operations at Guantanamo Bay on Cuba had been restricted.

Holmes and James were bundled off the aircraft, placed in separate cells and left to ponder their future treatment.

Chapter 54. Michelle: In Dubai

Michelle saw the emergency vehicles waiting on one of the taxiways leading onto the runway as the aircraft raced past them. She wondered if they would all have to exit via the escape slides. The upper deck, where she sat, was nearly twenty feet above the ground – about the same as a typical house roof. She'd tucked the document wallet containing her tickets, passport, phone and purse inside her jacket, its strap round her neck, so she wouldn't have to leave them behind if they did evacuate. As they came to a stop, the cabin crew stood by the exit doors ready to open them. The nearest one for her was a couple of rows further back.

She watched as some of the crews from the emergency vehicles disappeared under the massive wings while the vehicles aimed their foam nozzles towards the suspect engine. After a few minutes, the emergency vehicles pulled away from the Airbus and the aircraft started to taxi towards the terminal complex.

As requested, she remained in her seat while passengers who had been fortunate enough to be transferred onto other flights disembarked. When the cabin crew invited the rest of them to leave, she picked up her hand luggage and made her way to passport control.

This was a critical point.

If the money in Liechtenstein had been obtained illegally and the authorities knew of the misappropriation and if they suspected her, then presenting her passport might raise alarms. But what else could she do? She couldn't stay on board, she had to follow the other passengers. In any event, maybe they weren't looking for her. Maybe the money hadn't been obtained illegally or, if it had, maybe the company hadn't reported the loss.

Gradually the queue shuffled forward. The Immigration officer didn't seem to take much time over each passenger. Perhaps, knowing they were just in transit and hadn't expected to be in Dubai, they were only being subjected to a cursory check. She crossed her fingers for luck.

Three more before her.

Another was waved through, leaving two ahead of her.

Now just one.

Then it was her turn. She handed over the passport and looked straight at the officer. He glanced down at the passport then at her face then held the document against the electronic reader. He paused briefly then returned it to her.

"Next," he called.

Michelle pouched her cheeks and blew out from between pursed lips. She slipped the passport into her document wallet and looked for the staff who were shepherding the passengers who hadn't been allocated flights that day.

"We apologise for any inconvenience, ladies and gentlemen, we are flying in a replacement aircraft to take you on to London. We anticipate that this will be ready to depart at five o'clock this afternoon. In the meantime, we have arranged for you to be taken to a hotel where rooms have been reserved for you. We will collect you again at three. Please proceed through the exit where your coaches are waiting."

Michelle picked up her cabin bag and followed the crocodile of passengers outside. She took her seat on the second of the vehicles waiting for them. She was relieved to note that Holmes and James were not on the same coach. The transfer to the hotel took less than ten minutes and she was soon walking into the marble-floored reception area and collecting a room key.

She stripped off, had a quick shower then climbed, naked, into the bed as the dawn was breaking over the city. Laying there, Michelle thought back to the airport. As far as she could tell, the immigration officer had treated her exactly the same as everyone else – so had her concerns about the mysterious funds been groundless? Was it, somehow, legitimate? Perhaps she could use it. If so, how would she spend it? Half of it would buy a decent two-bedroom apartment – or, perhaps she could buy some properties to rent to secure her future.

Her phone alarm sounded at midday and she showered again and dressed using the change of underwear she habitually packed in her cabin luggage in case her main suitcase went astray.

Taking the lift down to the restaurant for breakfast, she felt less apprehensive than when she learned they were diverting to Dubai but she would be relieved to leave the UAE. Even dealing with Craig Mann's patronising attitude would be less stressful.

A representative of the airline came over to her as she ate the fresh fruit and yogurt she'd selected for her late breakfast.

"Miss Hartley, I'm glad to confirm that the flight to London is at five and the coaches will collect you at three. Once again, our sincere apologies for any inconvenience."

"Did you find out what the problem was?"

"Oh, I gather it seems to have been a defective temperature sensor – they found nothing wrong with the engine as such; so, no danger at all. But better safe than sorry, eh?"

"I suppose so. So, are we on the same aircraft?"

"No, as a precaution, they are replacing all of the sensors and that takes time."

Michelle drained her coffee cup, stood up and walked through the foyer to the lifts. She didn't see the man in a lightweight suit, carrying a briefcase, stop in his tracks and stare at her.

Back in her room, Michelle switched on the television to watch the international news. The fighting in Ukraine was still causing losses on both sides and the destruction of civilian areas. The UK continued to judder along as the various cliques in the so-called government continued their internecine battles for supremacy, the pound struggled to maintain parity with the Euro and the Dollar and interest rates remained high since the disastrous Truss administration. Perhaps she should emigrate to somewhere like New Zealand?

She was putting the last of her effects in the cabin case when there was a knock on the door.

Opening it, she was faced with two UAE police officers, a male sergeant and a female constable.

"Miss Hartley?"

"Yes."

"I am Sergeant Darwish. We require you to accompany us to the police station so that we can investigate a complaint that you embezzled money from your employer while you worked here."

Michelle's stomach dropped to the floor and her shoulders drooped.

"What are you on about? What's this about? I have a flight to catch at five o'clock, the coach is collecting us at three."

"I'm afraid you won't be on that plane."

Michelle realised she had no choice but to go with them.

"I demand to see someone from the British Embassy," she protested.

"Of course. That will be arranged."

Sergeant Darwish, gestured to his subordinate to pick up Michelle's case then opened the door.

At the police station, she was taken into an interview room. The woman police officer stood at the back of the room while the sergeant sat opposite Michelle at the table.

"We have sent for someone from the Embassy, but, while we wait, perhaps we can just complete some formalities," he said.

Michelle didn't say anything, she sat there nibbling her lower lip.

"Your full name is Michelle Samantha Hartley. Is that correct?"

She could hardly deny that was the case as he was holding her passport.

"Yes."

"You were born 24th November 1985?"

"Yes,"

"And you live at 1201 Harbour Towers, Salford in the United Kingdom?"

Michelle confirmed that was also correct.

"And you were employed by Marshall Investments in Dubai until thirtieth September twenty-twenty one?"

"Yes, why?"

"Mr Marshall alleges that you embezzled a large sum of money from his company."

"That's ridiculous. I've no idea why he'd make such an allegation. But I'm not saying anything else until I have legal representation from the embassy."

"That's your right, of course, but if you haven't anything to hide, why aren't you prepared to answer our questions?"

Michelle pursed her lips.

"I'm saying nothing until I have a chance to speak to someone from the embassy."

"Very well, in that case, you will be taken to a cell for the time being."

Before she was left in the cell, she was stripped of anything that she could use to harm herself then the door was slammed shut and the lock banged as it locked.

She sat on the bench that served as a bed and put her head in her hands.

'How strong was the evidence against her,' she wondered. If she'd been the real Michelle, she would have known what she'd done and be able to deal with questions. She could, of course, get out of the present situation by admitting she'd taken Michelle's identity – but that would leave her in trouble in the UK. Would the Dubai authorities pass that information to the UK? *'How could she prove she wasn't Michelle anyway – unless she admitted to being transgender.'* Then she'd be in trouble in the UAE for impersonating a woman as her female gender wouldn't be recognised. Mind you, that would probably carry less punishment than fraud. *'Did they cut off your hands for fraud like they did for stealing?'* she pondered.

Christ, this was a real mess and she was in it because a small component had failed on a five-hundred-million-dollar aircraft. She'd carefully planned her route to avoid any gulf states but all that planning had come to naught.

Chapter 55. Kilometre Eighteen

The base at Kilometre Eighteen was established after activities at Guantanamo Bay on Cuba had been exposed and successive presidents had promised to close it down. K18 was operated by a private company, allowing the Central Intelligence and Defence Intelligence Agencies to deny that they continued to use enhanced interrogation techniques on prisoners. Funding for the facility was buried in various military budgets. The base was also used for special forces training to cover the infrequent flights into the airfield and the cost of renting the base.

Ali sat in a room with two local interrogators.

"We know Holmes and James were responsible for the attack on the train. Frankly, I don't care about that, but they made it appear to have been carried out by believers to create more Islamophobia and that's blasphemy. The police in London didn't want to know about the evidence we provided – not surprising as their own investigations found the Metropolitan Police to be institutionally racist. They said our evidence was circumstantial. So, your job is to get confessions from them. Do what you need to do to get them."

Holmes looked up at the door when he heard a key being turned in the lock. Two guards entered the cell.

"Stand up," ordered the first. "Turn round and place your hands on the wall, shoulder-width apart."

Holmes stood his ground for a moment

"What's this about? Who are you? Where am I?" he demanded.

One guard struck him on his arm with his truncheon while the other watched him.

"Silence infidel. Do as you are told or you'll be punished."

Holmes' feet were dragged back – increasing the pressure on his arms and shoulders. A black hood was pulled over his head and headphones playing white noise dragged roughly onto his ears. He tried to stand upright but was forced back onto the wall. The opaque hood and sounds in his ears disorientated him and prevented him from knowing where the guards would hit next when they started to beat him. It wasn't a constant attack; part of the effectiveness was the pauses between strikes – the victim having no idea when the next strike would come or where.

After an hour, the guards dragged the headphones and hood off his head and left the cell. Holmes' relief at the removal of the headphones was short-lived. As the door clanged shut and the lock crashed across, the white noise started again through speakers in the top of the walls. The harsh white light was replaced with flashes from all angles.

Holmes tried to cover his eyes and ears to block out the bewildering combination.

Then the sprinklers in the ceiling sprayed him with cold water.

He lay shivering on the floor scared of what might be to come from the sub-humans that had kidnapped him.

James had been taken from his bare cell by two armed guards to the windowless interrogation room. The walls were whitewashed but grubby. Several rings were secured at shoulder height and about five feet apart in one wall. The concrete floor was stained in places. A hosepipe was attached to a single tap in one corner next to a board with retaining straps, lifted at one end. Overhead an exposed bulb cast a harsh light on the single table and two chairs in the centre of the room. The guards stood either side of the door while another male wearing a smart uniform entered the room and took one of the seats.

One of the guards roughly forced James into the chair opposite the nameless interrogator.

"Your name is Thomas James, is that correct?"

"What?" blustered James, his eyes widening as he took in the room and its contents.

"Answer our questions. Are you Thomas James, deputy leader of Action for England?"

"What? Yes, I am. What is this place? Why have I been brought here?"

"No questions. Tell us what we ask."

James was used to being the one demanding answers and using whatever force was necessary to persuade victims to respond. And, like all bullies, was a coward. He nodded his head, not daring to say anything.

"Do you know why we have brought you here?"

"No, No, I don't." James looked at the two guards in turn, then down at the floor. "Why am I here? It must be a mistake; I haven't done anything."

"What do you know about the bombing of the train from London to Manchester in October twenty-twenty-one?"

"Nothing, why would I?"

"You know nothing about the attack? You don't know a train was bombed? It was on the news and in the papers and your boss spoke about it on TV."

"Well, yes, I know a train was blown up and Peter Holmes was interviewed. It was blamed on a terrorist group." James refrained from being more specific about the ethnicity of the organisation blamed for the attack in view of those holding him prisoner.

"You surely know that Muslims were accused of the attack?"

"Well, yes, I did hear that."

"In fact, Holmes was specific in blaming true believers for the attack."

James tried to swallow but he'd had nothing to drink since they were on the Airbus and his throat was too dry.

"Yes, but..."

"But what? You know it wasn't Arabs who attacked the train. You know that because it was Action for England that organised the attack."

"What? No, of course not. We had nothing to do with it."

"Really?" the interrogator placed photographs on the desk and slid them across to James.

"Do you recognise this individual?"

James saw that it was Nathan Poulson walking past Singh's shop and entering the Nelson's Arms.

"I don't think so."

"I think you do. Perhaps a session on the board will refresh your memory."

The interrogator gestured to the guard and, together, they grabbed James by the arms and dragged him over to the plank by the tap in the corner. They forced him down onto it and secured his legs and wrists before lifting the end and resting it on a trestle with his feet higher than his head. The interrogator placed a cloth over James' face and poured water over it.

James couldn't breathe through the wet material which clogged his nostrils and mouth. He strained his hands against the restraints to try to reach the cloth and tear it off his face – but the straps held his wrists firmly; he shook his head from side to side to shake it loose – but the fabric remained moulded to his face. Feeling he was drowning, James tried to cry out.

"I'll tell you what you want to know," he mumbled through the cloth.

He was dragged back to the chair.

"Yes, I do recognise him. He was a member of Action for England. He came to see Holmes and me with a crazy idea of setting off a bomb and blaming it on an Arab group. Holmes and I wanted nothing to do with it and we sent him away."

"You sent him away? But we have evidence that he did set off the bomb."

The interrogator slid more photographs to James. They showed Poulson boarding the train at Euston. "The case he was pulling contained the bomb. What do you say to that?"

"If he did cause the explosion, it had nothing to do with Action for England."

"You want us to believe that?"

"It's the truth."

The interrogator shook his head.

"I don't think so. I think we need to give you more time to consider your story. We have as long as it takes. I can assure you, however, that it won't be pleasant for you."

Chapter 56. Michelle: Interrogation

Michelle had been left in her cell overnight. She'd tossed and turned, trying to decide how to respond to her situation.

Sergeant Homoud fetched her and took her back to the interview room. Lieutenant Maher was waiting for her together with a thirty-something woman wearing modest western dress.

"This is Miss Kent, from your embassy," Maher said.

Michelle nodded a greeting to her and received a forced smile in return.

"Miss Hartley, your employer, Mr Marshall, has made a complaint that while you were in his employ, you embezzled a large sum of money and had it transferred through a chain of numbered accounts to prevent it being traced."

"What are you talking about? I don't know anything about this." She screwed her forehead and looked straight into Maher's eyes, hoping her body language didn't betray how she was feeling.

Maher passed her a photograph of an orange USB memory stick.

"Do you recognise this?" he demanded.

"No, I've never seen it before," she replied honestly.

"We believe it contains the code that you set up on the system at Marshall's to provide you with a back door to allow you to make changes without it being recorded on the system log. It was found hidden in your old desk — taped to the bottom of one of the drawers."

"I don't know anything about it – and I wouldn't know how to write the code in any case."

"Don't take me for a fool. You're an IT expert. I'm sure you could create the application."

"I'm an IT Project Manager, I know how to manage teams of specialists – but it would be impossible for me to be expert at all the different tasks."

"Yet on your Curriculum Vitae, you claim to have experience of programming?"

"I did some basic courses in Oracle and C Plus a few years ago – sufficient to be able to understand what developers were talking about – but not enough to write the scripts myself. I may have given the impression that it was more than that on my CV – but everyone exaggerates on CVs."

"Well, no matter. There were very clear fingerprints and DNA samples on the memory stick and these are being compared with yours. We should have the results shortly. Why don't you make life easier and admit you took the money?"

Michelle realised that there was no possibility of the results incriminating her – even if the original Michelle had handled it.

"I'm glad to hear it. I've never handled the memory stick so unless the results are falsified, it will clear me."

Her response wasn't what Maher had expected. He was certain Michelle was hiding something which had convinced him of her guilt – especially with her flight plans.

"So, how do you explain how it came to be hidden in your old desk?"

"How should I know? I haven't been here for more than a year. Maybe Marshall is the one you should be questioning. Maybe his wife learned of his affairs. Maybe she's divorcing him and taking him to the cleaners. Maybe he siphoned off funds from the company and made it look like I was responsible because I turned down his advances. I don't know. How could I?"

Maher stroked his beard and stared at her.

If the fingerprints and DNA weren't hers, he doubted if he'd have a case. Avoiding the UAE wasn't a crime and being questioned by police often made people nervous and appear to be hiding something.

The door to the interview room opened and another officer looked in. He looked at Maher and shook his head.

Lieutenant Maher stood up and left the room for a few minutes.

"Miss Hartley, as you claimed, the DNA and fingerprints are not yours."

Michelle breathed a sigh of relief and started to stand up.

"I take it I'm free to leave then?" she asked.

"Not so fast. There is an anomaly with your DNA test. It shows XY chromosomes, not the XX that females have. Perhaps you'd care to explain how that can be?"

Chapter 57. A4E: Interrogation

The door to Holmes' cell opened as James was being dragged past. He could see the drenched state of his deputy and how his head slumped on his shoulders.

'What had they done to him, had he talked?' he wondered. *'If so, what had he told them?'*

An Arab wearing sand colour disruptive pattern material fatigues standing in the doorway pointed at Holmes.

"Out!" he ordered.

Holmes wearily put the palms of his hands on the bench to help him stand up. Not satisfied with the speed of his response, the soldier took two steps across the cell, grabbed him by the neck and pulled him towards the door.

"Faster. When we say move, you move immediately."

He pushed him through the door then down the corridor and into the interrogation room James had just vacated.

"Ah, Mr Holmes. Sit down please. Would you like a cigarette?" The interrogator asked genially – offering him the pack after taking one himself and lighting it.

"Now, what can you tell me about this man?" he asked, showing Holmes the photographs of Nathan Poulson.

'Had James told them who Poulson was? Had he said that he was a member of A4E? How much did the rag heads know? They must know something; getting him and James off the aircraft and away from Dubai had taken organisation and they wouldn't have done that unless they suspected him of involvement in the attack. Fuck, how much shit was he in? Was there a way out of it?'

"His name is Poulson, he used to be a member of Action for England. Why, what has he done?"

"You know exactly what he did. You organised it."

"Organised what? I don't know what you're talking about. If Poulson has done something, I know nothing about it. We have tens of thousands of members – I don't know what they all do in their private lives."

The interrogator leant across the table and slapped the cigarette from between Holmes' lips as he took another drag.

"Really, Holmes, don't take me for a fool. Your group has nothing like tens of thousands of members. It doesn't have two thousand even after the surge following the train bombing in 2021 – which was the motivation for the attack." The amiableness had been replaced by a chilly tone. "We know Action for England was behind the atrocity and that you made it look like it had been carried out by an Islamic group to attract new members."

Holmes shook his head, tried to shrink into himself and clasped his hands together to conceal the tremors. His chest tightened and he wondered if he was about to have a heart attack.

"What? No, no we had nothing to do with it. OK, I'll tell you the truth. Poulson came to James and me with that idea but we turned him down. As God is my witness, that's the truth. You have to believe me."

"You dare to blaspheme? What do you know of God? Do you even believe? Have you ever read the Koran?"

The interrogator leaned across the table so their faces were inches apart. The icy look in the questioner's stare sent a shiver down Holmes' spine. Holmes dropped his eyes, not daring to return the look; scared that the inquisitor would see into his soul and see the truth hidden there; he didn't even dare show his contempt for the Arab. He could feel pressure building in his bladder and prayed that he wouldn't wet himself.

"You will tell us the truth. It may be today, it may be tomorrow, it may be next week. But you will tell us what we want to know. How much you suffer in that time is entirely up to you."

Holmes remembered how James had been as they'd dragged him past his cell earlier. Could he tolerate what James had been put through? But what would happen to them if they admitted what they'd done? Would they be returned to England or tried and punished here? Or would they just quietly disappear? He'd heard of blasphemy being punished by beheading in parts of the Arab world – would that apply to him?

Could he convince them that Poulson had acted independently? Or, perhaps, blame James?

Chapter 58. Michelle: XY

M ichelle looked at Lieutenant Maher as he stared at her.

"Well? How do you explain how you have XY chromosomes when everyone knows females have XX? There are laws in this country about men impersonating women."

The embassy official who had been silently observing proceedings finally stepped in.

"Steady on Lieutenant Maher, there's no need to be offensive. I'm sure there will be another explanation. Perhaps we should have a doctor examine her. Would you have any objection, Miss Hartley?"

Michelle hesitated. *'Would a doctor be able to tell that she'd had surgery? Did she have any alternative to agreeing? What would happen if it was discovered that she was trans? Was there any way of telling when she'd transitioned? Could she claim to have done so years ago? Her passport was genuine and there would be a record of a birth certificate in Michelle's name. If she'd transitioned normally, there would have been a Gender Recognition Certificate but would the records be available to embassy officials?'*

"Miss Hartley? Are you prepared to be examined?" Lt Maher asked.

"What? This is ridiculous. I've no idea why the results show XY chromosomes. Maybe there was an error with the test?" she protested.

"If that's the case, then perhaps the comparison with the memory stick was also wrong. We will repeat the test," Maher announced triumphantly. "In the meantime, I will arrange for a doctor to examine you. You are hiding something Miss Hartley but I will discover what it is."

"Fine," Michelle spat out.

"Take her, or him whatever it is back to the cells," sneered Maher.

"I need some time in private with my client while we wait for the doctor," Hannah Kent told Maher.

"Very well, you can stay here for the moment, you'll have to be locked in. An officer will be in the corridor. He can let you out if necessary."

"So, Michelle, it's best if I know the full story if I'm to help you at all. The DNA tests are a double-edged sword. On the one hand, they exonerate you as far as the embezzlement is concerned – but they suggest that you're a man impersonating a woman in their eyes."

Michelle considered her options. She could tell the embassy official a version of the truth. She'd used Glen Hargreaves' identity when seeing the Gender Clinic and that formed part of the background for the hospital. She'd visited the town where he'd grown up and could probably answer questions about it. But, would that solve her situation – or replace it with another problem?

If she now claimed to be Australian, the British Embassy official wouldn't be interested in her case and she'd be passed over to their antipodean counterparts. She might then also face charges of using a false passport and, if she was eventually released and expelled from the UAE, it would be to Australia, not the UK. She might even be prevented from returning to Salford so lose access to her finances. She made up her mind.

"I didn't embezzle any money from Marshall's and I have never seen the USB stick before. I don't understand why the DNA says I have XY chromosomes. If that is the case, it must be one of those rare anomalies. I don't know, I'm not a geneticist. Do you want to check between my legs yourself? Would that satisfy you?"

Hannah Kent stared at Michelle. Her body language when talking about Marshalls and the memory stick suggested she was being honest. But when she denied knowing why she had XY chromosomes, the eyes flickered downwards and made her question her answer.

"OK, if that's how you want to play it, fine. I certainly don't want to examine you myself and I doubt if my word would be sufficient for Maher in any case. It'll have to be one of their doctors. I'll do what I can for you. I hope it's enough."

A key rattled in the lock and the door swung open again.

Maher entered accompanied by a white-coated woman with a stethoscope around her neck.

"This is Doctor Sindi. She will examine you. Miss Kent can stay or leave, it's your choice."

Michelle looked at Doctor Sindi. She appeared late thirties or early forties. Her blue Hijab covered her hair but left her face visible.

"Hello, Michelle, is it OK if I call you Michelle? I'm Dr Sindi. I gather the police want you me to examine you and confirm whether you have male or female genitalia. Are you happy for me to do that? Perhaps happy is the wrong word – I'm sure you are far from happy to be put through this."

"Let's just get on with it," Michelle snapped.

"Very well, but this room isn't at all suitable." She turned to the police officer, "Lieutenant Maher, please have Miss Hartley escorted to the medical room. I'll do the examination there."

Maher paused as if he was going to argue but turned and nodded to Sergeant Homoud and they followed Doctor Sindi down the corridor to the examination room. The sergeant remained on duty outside the office while Michelle, Miss Kent and the Doctor stepped into the room. Lieutenant Maher marched off down the corridor.

"Would you please go behind the screen, remove your skirt and knickers and lie down on the examination couch. Call me when you are ready," Dr Sindi instructed.

Michelle did as she was told and the doctor joined her.

"Could you open your knees apart for me please? Fine, thank you, you may get dressed again." With that, the doctor slipped through the screen and left Michelle on her own.

'Was that it?' Michelle wondered as she pulled her knickers back up and straightened her skirt. She caught sight of her image in a mirror over a sink and wished she had her make-up and a brush with her as she looked a mess after the night in the cell. Sighing, she pulled the curtain screen open and joined Sindi and Kent. The doctor was sitting at the desk and on the telephone, she gestured to Michelle to take the chair next to Hannah Kent.

"Lt Maher will join us in a minute but, to put your mind at rest, I shall be informing him that I found no evidence that you are a male dressed in female clothes."

Michelle suddenly felt light-headed and closed her eyes. She was glad she was already sitting down as she was sure her knees would have given way under her.

"Before he joins us, can I ask, when was your last period?"

Michelle might have anticipated such a question if there was a possibility that she was pregnant – but that could never happen.

Before she could think of an answer, there was a knock on the door and it opened to admit Maher.

"Well, doctor, what's the verdict? Is this person impersonating a female or not?" he demanded.

"I found no evidence to indicate that Miss Hartley is anything other than the woman she appears to be."

"But how can that be? She he has XY chromosomes and that means they are male. If they were female, they'd have XX chromosomes," he blustered.

"It's not as simple as that," Dr Sindi said. "There are several other factors that can result in anomalies including some that can result in an individual having XY chromosomes but female genitalia and breasts. I was just investigating one possibility when you came in. It's known as Androgen Insensitivity Syndrome. It occurs when the individual has XY chromosomes but the body is insensitive to the effects of testosterone during foetal development so the male sex organs don't develop."

Lieutenant Maher hooded his eyes and stroked his beard.

"You say Miss Hartley has male chromosomes but appears female. So, is she male or female?"

"The question you asked me to resolve was, is she a male impersonating a female? She was identified as female at birth, brought up as female, she looks female, she has been accepted as female, her passport and other documents list her as female. So, no, she is not a male impersonating a female."

Maher nodded his head.

"Very well, Miss Hartley it would appear that there is no evidence of you being involved in the embezzlement at Marshalls and as you haven't committed any other offences in the Emirates, you are free to leave. No doubt Miss Kent can assist in getting you back to your hotel then on to the airport."

Hannah Kent signalled her agreement with the tilt of the head.

"Before you go, I'd like another word with you in private, Michelle. Perhaps you could wait for her at reception, Miss Kent?" said Dr Sindi.

Once the others had left the room, the doctor turned to Michelle.

"Can I ask, do you have periods?" she asked.

Michelle thought before answering.

"The reason I ask is that AIS or Swyer syndrome means you wouldn't have female reproductive organs so wouldn't have periods. In fact, the conditions are usually identified while investigating the absence of periods or not being able to conceive. I'm afraid if you do have AIS or Swyer's, you won't be able to have children. I'm very sorry. There is also a risk of cancer developing with Swyer's – so I'd strongly recommend that you seek medical advice when you get back to the UK."

"Thank you, doctor. As it happens, I'm not that interested in having children the way the world is today so that's not a huge loss for me. Maybe I'll settle for a cat."

Chapter 59. Confessions

Holmes and James spent uncomfortable nights in their cells —exactly as their captors intended. Sleep deprivation was a tried and tested interrogation method.

Throughout the night white noise penetrated all of their senses, not only their hearing. If they covered their ears with their hands, the flashing lights pierced their eyelids and sent overpowering signals through their optic nerves. There were breaks in these assaults but Holmes and James didn't know how long those respites would last. The first time the noise and lights ceased, they hoped they'd have a chance to rest at least for a few minutes. Then cold water sprayed them from the ceiling.

Shivering afterwards, the concrete slabs that served as beds felt even harder than before. The rough surface dug into their skin and, if they tried adjusting their position, scratched them through their sodden clothes.

Holmes heard James being dragged along the corridor. A few minutes later, the door to his own cell opened and the guard grabbed his arm and pulled him along to an interrogation room. He was pushed inside and forced into a seat next to a table. On one wall was a large monitor showing another interrogation room. The other room was identical to the one Holmes was in. He realised the prisoner sitting at the table was his deputy. As he watched, one of the guards plugged a lead into a device then attached the crocodile clip at the other end to James' right nipple. As it bit into the skin, Holmes shivered at how it must feel. The guard then plugged a second lead into the device then bent over James and attached it somewhere between his legs. Although Holmes couldn't actually see where it was, he just knew it would be on his deputy's genitalia.

'*Christ,*' he thought, '*Tommy looks bad.*' His face was swollen, his shirt was torn in several places and it looked as though the buttons had been ripped open leaving James' chest exposed. There were red marks on his skin. '*Had they used lit cigarettes on him?*' he wondered. The interrogator was certainly smoking and drinking a coffee. '*God, what I'd do for a drink, my throat is parched*'.

As he stared at James, the door to his own room opened and his inquisitor from the day before entered. He looked refreshed and was dressed in a smartly pressed uniform bearing the three pips of a captain on his epaulettes. A woman carrying a tray with a coffee pot and cups and saucers followed him into the room. The officer gestured for her to put the tray on the table. He then turned to the prisoner.

"Good morning, Mr Holmes, I trust you slept well. No? Well, the solution is in your own hands. Tell us what we want to know and you can leave. Remain obstinate and you continue to enjoy our hospitality," he told Holmes as he poured himself a cup of the fine-ground, unfiltered infusion and took a sip.

"But I'm forgetting my manners. Would you like some coffee?"

Holmes was reluctant to show any weakness but the aroma had set off his olfactory senses, he yearned for the anticipated taste and refreshing hit it would bring. The captain filled the second cup then set it in front of Holmes.

"Now, isn't that more civilised? Unfortunately, I fear Mr James is taking a more stubborn approach. Such a shame. Don't you want to help your friend? Answer our questions and we'll put both of you on a flight back to the UK. It's your choice."

At that moment, Holmes saw James convulse, his head thrown backwards as the interrogator in the other room threw a switch on the device he was holding.

James' screams were muffled by the intervening walls.

"I dislike hearing another human being suffering, don't you Mr Holmes? So, I have the sound muted. Of course, I could provide you with headphones so that you can listen in if you wish?" It was said in such a matter-of-fact manner – as though they were discussing the finer points of a game of football.

The captain snapped his fingers and the guard who'd been standing by the door took the headphones from the captain and put them over Holmes' ears. As he did so, the interrogator in the other room activated the device once more and James let out a piercing scream that penetrated Holmes' entire being.

'Could he put up with what Tommy James was being subjected to?' he wondered. He doubted it. *'What would happen to them if he did give in to the torture? Would they be released? That seemed unlikely, or would they be detained in this fly-infested excuse for a country? What would the jails be like? How would they be treated?'* He didn't even want to consider those options. But what were the alternatives?'

"Come Peter, you don't mind me calling you Peter, I trust," the captain said as he smacked his lips and returned his coffee cup to its saucer. "You surely don't want to suffer the same as Tommy, do you? But that will be the price for silence."

He lit a cigarette and blew the harsh smoke in Holmes' direction. It wasn't the aromatic product of one of his cigars, but it triggered his yearning for nicotine.

"We know what you did to the train. It was a clever scheme. As for the victims, they were no friends of ours; but blaming the attack on an Islamic group was unforgivable and you will be punished for that heresy. And you will make it clear where the blame really lay. Do that and you can live."

Holmes dropped his chin and stared at his hands holding the coffee cup, unwilling to look his interrogator in the eyes.

'If he did as they demanded, and they were returned to the UK, what would the consequences be?' Holmes wondered. 'Presumably, the Arabs would provide recordings of the confessions. Could James and he retract them as having been extracted under torture? Would that convince everyone? Would it convince anyone? Confessions obtained in that way would not normally be admissible in UK courts and he had friends in the Police and Crown Prosecution Service who could be relied on to question their use. With luck, he and James would avoid prison. Well, he probably could. If necessary, he could always shift all the blame onto Nathan Poulson and, if that wasn't enough, he could claim that Tommy had acted independently. OK, that might result in an English prison for his deputy but Holmes would have saved him from serving time here or possibly execution. He ought to be grateful for that.

'The general public was another matter. Maybe some would resent being misled about who had set off the bomb, especially as he'd gone on TV to blame Islamic terrorists. Others might congratulate him on the way they'd built resentment against immigrants. Some of A4E's members would still believe the original story and claim he had been forced to falsely confess to the attack to prevent further torture.'

Holmes lifted his eyes, blinking away tears of shame as he was forced to submit.

"What do you want me to tell you?" he asked in barely more than a whisper.

"The truth. How you came up with the idea, how you selected Poulson to carry out the attack, where you met, how and where the bomb was made and where you got the components, how the attack was carried out."

Holmes knew he had no choice if he wanted to live.

Chapter 60. Michelle Returns Home

Michelle breathed a sigh of relief as the Airbus raced down the runway and climbed over the Persian Gulf. A helpful customer services agent had transferred her to a direct flight back to Manchester. She hoped she'd never have to repeat the experience of the last couple of days ever again.

She'd learned in her biology classes at school that women had XX chromosomes and men had XY – but hadn't heard of other variations, including those mentioned by Doctor Sindi. She'd fully expected to have to admit to being transgender to explain the discrepancy. Thankfully, the complications that Dr Sindi had warned against wouldn't apply to her. As for having children, she had Charlotte and Jessica though she'd never be able to see them again. She looked at her watch – quarter to three, so quarter to eleven in the UK; they'd almost certainly be at the stables practising jumping for the next gymkhana. Did they still think of their dad – or had they totally moved on? She hoped they hadn't been badly affected by her 'death' but that they still thought of him – it would have to be Michelle's male past that they remembered.

It was a dark wet evening when they landed in Manchester. Thankfully, it didn't take too long to clear passport control and collect her baggage. As she passed through the terminal, she noticed a small supermarket and realised that there would be nothing to eat or drink at the flat so she picked up a few essentials before joining the taxi queue.

"Good trip?" the driver asked as he pulled onto the M56 and the spray from passing traffic reduced visibility to a few yards.

"Interesting and varied," Michelle replied. There had certainly been absolute extremes – the surgery that had corrected her birth defect, as she saw it, at one end and the police interrogation at the other – and some fabulous experiences during her tours of Thailand and Australia in between.

She took out her phone and accessed her Hive app. She'd left the apartment heating on low to prevent frozen pipes while away but it was time to bring it up to a more comfortable level.

Notwithstanding the rain, the familiar sights were comforting as they joined the M60 ring road then down the slip road onto the A56. She'd breathed a sigh of relief when the aircraft took off from Dubai – but it was only now that she felt truly safe.

At the flat, she paid off the cabbie and wheeled her suitcase into the entrance lobby. She collected her mail and took the lift to her floor. Once inside the flat, she put away the shopping she'd bought at the airport and, while the coffee brewed in the cafetière, unpacked, sorted her laundry and put a first batch into the washing machine.

Adding a dash of milk to her mug she took her coffee into the lounge and sorted through the mail. There was nothing that needed her immediate attention. The bank statement for her current account showed a healthy balance even after the heavy expenditure on her trip; the credit card of just under five thousand would be paid in full automatically. There was a Christmas card from Zoë with a message saying she hoped Michelle was enjoying Christmas 'wherever she was', a circular from the local Labour MP and one from the Lib-Dems who had one of the three councillors representing the Quays ward. The bank statements went into her 'shred' tray, the rest into the paper recycling.

Sitting back in her seat, coffee mug in her hands she pondered whether to have a simple meal, perhaps poached egg on toast or an omelette, or walk over to one of the restaurants at Media City for dinner. The omelette with buttered toast spread with Marmite won.

Although it was only nine pm in the UK, Michelle's body clock, still on Dubai time, told her it was one am and she was ready for her bed. If she gave way, however, she knew she'd wake too early the next morning so she fought the temptation to undress and slip between the sheets. Instead, she put on the news.

"Concern is being raised about the whereabouts of Peter Holmes and Tommy James of Action for England," the newsreader intoned. "They were last seen on a Qantas flight that diverted to Dubai last week after engine problems. Most of the other passengers returned on a replacement aircraft the following day but Holmes and James were not on board. They do not appear to have made use of the hotel rooms arranged for them while waiting for the replacement flight. Officials in Dubai say there is no record of them having entered the UAE. A statement from the Foreign and Commonwealth Office reports that that the local embassy is investigating the issue."

The last Michelle had seen of the pair was when they entered the Business Class area at the front of the aircraft while she'd taken her place further back in the fuselage. Not that she particularly cared what had happened to the two bigots.

Drooping eyelids eventually overcame her wish to stay up later. So, she undressed, showered, set her alarm clock for the morning and read for a few minutes before settling further down in the bed and switching off the light.

The next morning, forty-five minutes before her usual start time, she entered the familiar office block.

It had been eight weeks since she'd started her break and she wondered what news waited for her. She booted up her computer then logged into her emails. As expected, there were dozens of unread messages. Most would be CC'd to her for information; she'd go through those more carefully later when she'd checked those that might need action.

There were no disasters as far as she could see. The building works were, unsurprisingly, three weeks behind schedule which meant the next stage of her project would be affected – but that could have been much worse.

There were delays, too, on orders for some of the equipment required for the server room. That could have meant her project being blamed for the setback if it hadn't been for the over-run on the building works – now it wouldn't matter.

She scheduled a project team meeting for immediately after lunch so she could be brought up to date on the individual workstreams.

Her early start meant she'd made good inroads into the emails before her colleagues started to arrive and demanded to hear about her trip. Even Sylvia Farrell, her boss, wanted the details and insisted that they had coffee together in her office.

"There's no panic over the project as the construction company is running late," Sylvia pointed out, "we can afford a catch-up. So, come on, spill the beans – any holiday romances in the mysterious east?"

Michelle surrendered to the inevitable and showed Sylvia some of the photographs she'd taken. She realised, however, that if she was going to get any work done that afternoon, she'd need to take control and send a group email inviting any of the project team who were interested to join her for drinks after work. The ploy worked and she was able to focus on the tasks she needed to prioritise that week.

They assembled around their usual 'Friday night' table in the bar and Michelle set up her laptop so she could show the photographs and videos from her trip. The others ooh'd and aah'd at the sights – especially the firework display over Sydney Harbour Bridge. Gradually the team made their excuses and left for home leaving just Zoë, Linda, Sylvia and Michelle.

"Anyone fancy dinner?" Michelle suggested.

"I can't," said Sylvia. "I've got a personal trainer booked at the gym in half an hour. So I'd better dash."

"Sorry, nor can I," added Linda.

Michelle looked at Zoë, "Don't tell me, you're off down the Village."

"What, on a Monday night? Not likely, it'll be dead. No, I'm up for a meal. Are you paying?"

"Yes, why not, last of the holiday spends. Where do you fancy?"

"How about the Italian?"

"Suits me."

Chapter 61. Holmes and James

Captain Khalid Ali stood in front of Colonel Malik's desk.

"Holmes has confessed. I have a written statement from him," Ali said, passing a copy to Colonel Malik. "We will video him reading it out and answering questions – he is being cleaned up and provided with fresh clothes from his own luggage. I am confident when James sees that Holmes has confessed, he will do the same. I'm afraid his treatment has left a few marks so we will have to leave filming him for the time being."

"Excellent. Well done, Captain. The question is whether the British will believe the confessions. They didn't want to know about the information we provided before."

"True but Holmes has admitted to specific details that he could only know if he'd been involved. We also have agreement from our cousins across the border to bring pressure on the UK government to use the information we provide or face difficulties over orders for the sixth-generation fighter aircraft. They hope our neighbours will replace their Eurofighter Typhoons with the Tempest at the end of the decade. I doubt Prime Minister Sunak will risk more than twenty billion pounds worth of orders for the sake of Holmes and James."

Malik nodded his head.

"Very good Ali. If the confessions do their job, you can look forward to promotion to Major."

Ali brought his feet together, saluted, smartly about-faced and marched out of the room.

Holmes had been moved from the forbidding interrogation room to a more comfortable, well-decorated office with a desk and a chair. Aimed at the chair was a professional video camera mounted on a sturdy tripod and lights. He was surprised to note that there were no flags or other symbols representing his captors to claim credit for his confession. Instead, the background was a plain wall. Behind the camera were two other chairs.

The operator was adjusting something on the equipment, his guard stood by the door, a third man placed a bottle of water and some paper cups on the desk. He indicated to Holmes to take the seat, then adjusted the lights as directed by the cameraman.

Ali entered the room and handed Holmes a copy of his confession.

"You will read your statement – I will then ask additional questions. Is that understood?"

"Yes, it is," Holmes replied wearily.

Ali turned to the crew and asked a question of each, which Holmes assumed was to ensure they were ready to proceed.

Holmes was aware that forces' personnel who were at risk of capture underwent training to provide signals during filming to convey messages to potential rescuers or to indicate that they were being coerced into making their confession, but he hadn't had that training and, in any event, he didn't imagine for one moment that the UK government would risk anyone to rescue James or him.

Recording his statement took half an hour with another fifteen minutes of additional questioning. Ali kept out of shot for the session so there was nothing to identify where they were or who had abducted the Action 4 England pair.

Following the recording, Holmes was returned to a cell.

"I said that if you cooperated, you would be treated better," Ali reminded him as he was shown into a space that wouldn't qualify for any hotel stars but was much more comfortable than his previous accommodation.

In place of the concrete bench that had served as a bed were two frames with mattresses. They were lumpy; probably stuffed with hay or straw but it was a huge improvement. And there were blankets. They might be thinner than any he'd seen before but they were better than nothing. Along one wall was a table and two chairs and, behind a screen in one corner, a toilet and wash basin rather than the galvanised bucket of the previous cell. Holmes looked at the ceiling. As far as he could tell, there were no sprinklers and no drain in the floor, so perhaps he would be spared the icy showers.

"How much longer are you holding us?" Holmes asked.

"That depends on your government and how quickly Mr James recovers from his treatment. We don't want to give the impression that we've been less than hospitable."

"What's happening to Tommy James?" asked Holmes. "Is he OK?"

"You can see for yourself very shortly; he will be joining you here. You know that, unlike yourself, he resisted our questioning and suffered the consequences. You will both be held until his bruising subsides."

As Ali finished speaking, the door opened and James was brought into the room restrained on each side by guards. They dragged him to one of the beds and pushed him onto it. He fell backwards and hit his head on the wall. Ali yelled something at the guards which Holmes took to be a rebuke from his tone.

Ali turned to Holmes. "Clumsy oafs, we don't want to cause your colleague any more injuries. Now, I have arranged food for you. It will be here soon. I will also have a change of clothes brought for Mr James."

Captain Ali then left the cell; Holmes went over to his deputy who was slumped on the bed. James' face was splattered with blood from his beatings. Holmes looked around for something with which he could clean him up but there was nothing but the clothes they wore and the blankets on the beds. James' shirt had been torn during his interrogation so Holmes ripped off a handkerchief-sized piece and wet it from the basin tap.

As he cleaned his face, James started to come round.

"Peter. Is that you? Are you OK? What's happening to us? I didn't say a thing about Nathan Poulson and the crash."

"We'll be all right now. They made me watch, I had to tell them the truth to stop them torturing you. They forced me to write a confession then the bastards videoed me reading it." Holmes paused and looked around hoping no microphones were recording his indiscreet comment about their captors. "They say they're going to give it to the UK authorities, but they won't be able to use it in court as it was obtained under duress," he continued.

"So, what happens now?"

"They're keeping us here while your injuries heal, then they'll send us back to England. At least we're still alive."

"Looks like you got off fucking lightly. As usual, I got the shitty end of the stick." James snarled.

"I guess they thought I'd do more to protect you than avoid being tortured myself. Would it have helped if they treated me the same way?"

James curled his lips and stared into Holmes' eyes. Unable to return his deputy's glare, Holmes looked away.

"Do you want some water?" he asked, trying to change the subject. "I'm afraid the catering doesn't run to Napoleon brandy." He stood up and walked over to the table and poured him a cup.

James gingerly sipped at the water, his cut lips and bruised jaw making movement painful.

"So, what did you say in your effing confession? How much trouble is it going to cause us?"

"They already knew a lot so I couldn't bluff them. I tried at first to blame Poulson but they'd worked out that he didn't have the intelligence to organise it on his own."

"And is that when you tried to shift it onto me?" James accused.

"What? No, I never did any such thing. How could you think I'd do that? Come on Tommy, how long have we worked together? Surely you know me better than that."

"It's because I do know you so well, Peter, that I know you'd have no hesitation throwing me to the wolves if you thought it might save your own skin. But it is what it is. Can our friends in the police or the CPS help kill the case? Or are we likely to face a trial?"

"I'm not sure. They were able to suppress the Habbani reports last year – but if they put the video out on the internet, it will make life very difficult."

"Difficult for you or for both of us? Just what did you say about my involvement?"

"I had to tell them that you made the detailed arrangements and organised the suitcase bomb. They wouldn't have believed me if I'd said I'd done it."

James shook his head.

"No, they wouldn't. You're the speaker, the rabble-rouser but you couldn't organise a proverbial piss-up in a brewery. That's why you've always needed me."

"I don't deny it and we've worked well together as a team. I'm sorry it's come to this. I don't think they'll use the video online initially if they want to see us in court. Our briefs would be able to challenge the CPS over whether we could get a fair trial if everyone had seen the confession. We'll try to get it disbarred. We're not done for yet. We might even be able to raise funds for our defence and recruit more members."

Chapter 62. Michelle: Flat Share

As the waiter left, having taken their order, Michelle saw Zoë staring at his bottom weaving its way between the tables. Realising she was being watched, she smiled and raised her eyebrows.

"Nice bum," she said with a sigh.

"You sound down," Michelle remarked.

"You'd probably be the same. I've been on the waiting list for the Gender Clinic now for more than two years. There's a new interim service in Manchester – but it's still likely I'll have to wait at least another three years before I can get surgery. And I just can't wait that long. I've got to do something sooner or I don't know what I'll do. Well, I do know and I don't want to go that route. This damned government treats us like shit. There were plans to make getting a Gender Recognition Certificate easier – Theresa May's government even had it in their programme. Then it was dumped by that clown of a mini-Trump we had along with plans to outlaw conversion therapy for trans people. They're banning it for lesbians and gays but need to think more about trans folks. Makes me sick."

"Isn't the Scottish government making it easier to get a GRC with self-identification?"

"Yes, they are. If Westminster lets them get away with it. But that doesn't deal with the issues of long waiting lists."

"I suppose not. I realise you shouldn't have to go privately, but is that an option for you?"

"Have you any idea what that costs? And it's not just the surgery. If you go to, say, Thailand, you need to allow for recuperation afterwards before flying home. Anyway, that's my problem, not yours – unless you've got a spare twenty grand you can lend me."

Michelle reflected that she'd been very fortunate that she'd inherited her predecessor's bank balances as well as her identity. She *could* easily lend Zoë money for surgery – there was still nearly a hundred and twenty-five thousand in the deposit account let alone the one and a half million in Liechtenstein.

"I was saving three hundred a month but they've put the rent up on my apartment and my flatmate has moved out so I'm having to dip into my surgery fund," Zoë added. "I might have to find somewhere cheaper – if I can find someone willing to share with a trans woman."

The waiter came back to their table with the bottle of wine they'd ordered. He poured a little into Michelle's glass and waited for her to taste it.

"That's fine," she confirmed. Once their glasses had been charged, they clinked them together.

"Cheers," they said in harmony.

Taking a segment of garlic bread, Michelle looked across the table. She felt sorry for Zoë's plight and would like to help her if possible. She wasn't at all religious – and didn't believe she'd be judged for her earthly behaviour. If that was the case, she'd be in trouble for having taken Michelle's identity even though that, itself, hadn't hurt anyone else. Well, providing she ignored the effect on her two girls – but they'd have been hurt even more if she'd gone down any other of the routes she'd had available at the time. She did have some vague belief in Karma and that good and bad deeds brought their own consequences.

She'd been in the right place at the right time when the train crashed – perhaps she needed to pay forward some of that good fortune and help Zoë. Maybe she needed to see how she could use the one and a half million pounds in Liechtenstein to support other trans people. It was the only link with the funds embezzled from Marshall Investments. She was quite certain that if she tried to use that money for her own benefit, it would come back and bite her. Use it for charitable work without any link to her and she'd still be comfortable and safe.

The issue was how to help Zoë without raising questions that might expose her own history.

"So, come on, tell me about your holiday, I know you said you were heading for South East Asia, but where did you actually go? And how many holiday romances did you have?" Zoë demanded.

Michelle took a sip of wine before answering to give herself time to recall the timeline she'd worked out to conceal the week in hospital.

"My original plan was to spend the first couple of weeks in Thailand. My grandfather was a prisoner of war of the Japanese and worked on the death railway so I wanted to visit the museum and pay my respects to his comrades who died. I'd also found a floating hotel on the River Kwai and I spent a few days there. They don't use power so everything is lit by paraffin lights. It was very atmospheric. You get there in these 'long tail' boats that skim across the water."

Michelle was able to produce photographs of this stage of her trip but had to gloss over the invented parts, scuba diving off the coast, using some of the dive operators' own website photographs of the boat and fish.

"Didn't you plan to take a motorbike through Cambodia and Vietnam? Did you get to Angkor Wat?"

"Unfortunately, no. There were still Covid restrictions in place so I had to change my plans. I flew down to Australia early instead."

"So, what about your love life? Don't tell me you didn't have a fling or two."

Michelle gave Zoë a slightly modified version of her encounter with Clifford Miller, the American she'd met in Pattaya.

After dinner, they walked back to Harbour City metro stop where Zoë caught the tram back home and Michelle went into her apartment block and took the lift to her floor. Inside her flat, she hung up her coat, kicked off her shoes and made a cup of coffee. Sipping the strong dark liquid, she thought again about Zoë's dilemma.

She felt there were three options. Do nothing, offer Zoë a loan or offer to share the flat. Or a combination of the loan and flat share.

Before having her operation, she wouldn't have considered sharing in case her genitals were accidentally exposed. Now that didn't matter. She enjoyed Zoë's company; they shared some interests and it would be great to have someone to chat to in the evenings. The flat was large enough for both of them – they'd just need to establish a few ground rules.

She decided to sleep on the question.

The next morning, Michelle had made up her mind. In the office, she called Zoë and asked if she could spare a couple of minutes in one of the small conference rooms.

"What's the problem, Michelle?" Zoë asked as she closed the door behind her.

"You said last night you needed to reduce your rent costs as your flatmate had moved out and the rents had gone up?"

"Yes, why? Do you know someone looking for somewhere?"

"Could be. What are you looking to pay?"

"It was nine hundred a month between us before Caz moved out. It's going up to a thousand and she didn't want to pay the extra fifty especially with gas and electricity costs rocketing. I don't want to pay more than four-fifty if I can. Everything over that comes off my surgery savings."

"How's that going?"

Zoë screwed up her eyes.

"Why the questions? What's on your mind?"

"How do you fancy sharing with me? Five hundred a month including power and internet."

"Really? Are you sure? That'd be fantastic."

Zoë took Michelle into her arms and hugged her tightly.

"That'll make such a huge difference – you can't imagine what it means to me. I might even be able to afford surgery this year even if I have to take out a bank loan for the balance."

"Come over this evening and we'll sort out the details," Michelle said knowing exactly how important the opportunity was to Zoë.

Chapter 63. Ali: Detained

Ali's flight from Dubai landed in London on time and he soon cleared passport control. As he only had hand luggage, it took little time to clear customs. An hour later he was in the reception area of Thames House, the Security Service's HQ close to Lambeth Bridge where he was to meet a Case Officer he'd worked with previously and hand over the information about Holmes and James.

Andrea Gibbs waved to Ali as she approached.

"Good to see you again, Khalid, come on through," she instructed.

He passed through the security barrier and followed her as she led the way.

"I've booked a room for our chat. My boss, Ruth Fleming, is going to sit in; I hope that's OK?"

Ali never knew whether the names he was given were genuine or not. Would they create a false name using one of the most famous spy thriller writers? But, if it was her real name, he was sure it would be the butt of jokes.

"Of course, no problem."

"So, Mr Ali, what do you have for us?" asked Ruth Fleming after they'd been introduced.

"Is this the stand-alone laptop for me to use?" he asked.

"Yes, it is," Andrea said. "Sorry we couldn't let you bring your own equipment or have your files loaded onto our servers. Would you like a coffee?"

"That's fine and yes please," he said, knowing that the coffee would be insipid compared with the way it was prepared in Habbani but it was, nevertheless, welcome.

The laptop was already plugged in and live and after Andrea had run a virus check on his memory stick, he soon accessed the files he wanted to display.

He quickly ran through the information about the bombing itself. The video clearly identified Nathan Poulson joining the train at Euston – then showed earlier shots of him going past Amar Singh's before crossing the road to the Nelson's Arms and, later, with Tommy James. He then ran the video of Holmes' confession and handed over the typed and signed copies.

Andrea and Fleming exchanged glances at the end of the video.

"There is no doubt that this proves that Action 4 England was responsible for the bombing – there are, however, a lot of legal questions that the lawyers will argue over including whether or not we can use a confession obtained outside the UK," Ruth Fleming told Ali.

"I realise that, but it gives yourselves or the police leads they can follow up to build their own case – especially around the manufacturing of the bomb. In any event, even if you don't get a conviction on a technicality, hopefully it will prove it wasn't an Islamic group that was responsible and it'll destroy Action 4 England's credibility."

"Maybe, though some A4E members will probably admire Holmes and James for blaming others," Andrea added.

"How long can you continue to hold them while we handle things this end?" Fleming asked.

"As long as you need, I suppose, though no doubt they'll protest about it when we hand them over."

"Give us a week, can you? I'll take the case upstairs and no doubt the chief will want to talk to the Home Secretary."

"That's fine with us so long as something is done this time. When I first provided information about A4E's involvement, Scotland Yard didn't want to know. Bear in mind that our neighbours are looking at placing big defence contracts with the UK and would prefer to deal with countries that are friendly rather than obstructive. They'd be unhappy if the case was simply buried. You may care to pass that on."

"We get the message Mr Ali; I think I can assure you that action will be taken this time." Ruth Fleming said.

The following Tuesday, Holmes and James were taken from the detention centre to the airstrip where the stubby Skyvan sat under the blazing sun. James' bruises had faded by now but he still limped as they were escorted from the SUV to the aircraft.

They were bundled inside the sparsely equipped fuselage. Behind them, the crew closed the rear cargo door and, as they took their seats, the two engines started to spin. A few minutes later they had taxied to the end of the short airstrip, the engines were run up to maximum power and the pilot released the brakes. The propellors created a sandstorm behind them as they trundled down the dirt runway becoming airborne after little more than four hundred yards.

Half an hour later, they approached Dubai where they had to circle while waiting for a landing slot. The international airliners left a great deal of turbulence in their wake which could flip the

Skyvan on its back so they needed to leave a long gap between the airliners and themselves.

Eventually, they pulled up outside the Habbani Aviation facility where they'd been detained two and a half weeks earlier. Holmes and James were hustled from the Skyvan to the office. A man and a woman in their thirties, the man dressed in a suit more appropriate to London's weather than the local heat, the woman in a more suitable blouse and skirt stood just inside.

"Peter Holmes and Thomas James, I'm Detective Inspector Collier, this is Detective Sergeant Page," the woman announced. "You are being extradited to the UK in connection with charges related to terrorist activities. The exact charges will be put to you in London."

DI Collier signed the document that the Habbani guards had presented to her accepting responsibility for the two prisoners. Holmes and James were then handcuffed to Collier and Page and led back outside.

Two ubiquitous four-by-fours with darkened windows waited with their engines running to power the air-conditioning. The prisoners and escorts shuffled into their seats, Collier and Holmes in the leading vehicle, Page and James in the other to prevent them talking to each other. Satisfied their passengers were safely on board, the drivers set off in convoy around the perimeter track, pausing only to obtain clearance to cross the runways.

They pulled up next to a gate servicing one of the Airbus 380s. They climbed the stairs of the airbridge and were led into the economy plus cabin where the seats were in pairs. They sat with Collier and Holmes on the port side and Page and James on the starboard side. The police officers taking the aisle seats trapping their charges next to the windows.

When the cabin crew came round with drinks, Collier accepted a soft drink while Holmes asked for a glass of wine.

"Make the most of it," Collier told him. "You won't be having any more for a very long time when you're back in the UK."

As the aircraft pulled up at the stand at London's Heathrow airport, Page held back to allow Holmes and Collier to disembark first. As they made their way to the exit, they passed several rows of experienced first-class passengers who knew better than to rush to reclaim their carry-on bags. They did, however, attract some curious looks as they'd made their way forward.

Once the door opened, Collier led Holmes along the airbridge to an electric buggy which whisked them ahead of the other passengers. She glanced back to confirm that Page and James were following in a second buggy. Inside the main terminal, they were dropped near Immigration and taken into private offices.

Detective Inspector Collier faced Holmes across the office.

"Peter Holmes, you have been arrested under the Terrorism Act 2000. You will be taken from here to Belmarsh Prison where you will be held while our investigations continue," she informed him. *"You do not have to say anything. But it may harm your defence if you do not mention when questioned something which you later rely on in court. Anything you do say may be given in evidence."*

In the next office, Page was performing the same ritual with Tommy James.

"What are the exact charges?" Holmes demanded to know. "When can I see a solicitor?"

"You will be advised of the exact charges in due course. We will arrange for you to see your solicitors when you get to Belmarsh."

The vehicle carrying Holmes passed through Belmarsh's outer gates and paused while they were closed behind it and the inner gates opened.

"Welcome to Hellmarsh," the driver said as they drove into the yard. "Like Colditz Castle in the war, it's been designed to be escape proof – unlike Colditz, no one has managed to escape from here."

Before being allowed out of the vehicle, he was double shackled – his wrists were handcuffed together and he was then handcuffed to a prison officer.

Another officer with a German Shepherd dog waited to escort him into the reception block. Between the buildings, Homes could make out the inner security fence and, beyond it, the outer wall that he estimated was at least twenty feet high with its rounded top. He hardly had time to take in the oppressive view before his escorts hustled him through the first of the doors and gates he'd encounter.

Inside, he was relieved of all his possessions and strip-searched, including intimate body cavities, before being processed and entered onto p-NOMIS the Prison Service's National Offender Management Information System.

He was eventually escorted to a cell and the door slammed shut behind him. He looked around his new home. There was a bunk bed, though he wasn't sharing at this time, a table and chair, a sink and toilet behind a screen to at least provide a little privacy.

When Holmes was finally able to see his solicitor, he pressed him about the admissibility of the confession he'd given in Habban.

"Surely we have contacts in the police or the CPS to have it thrown out, don't we?"

"Unfortunately, most of them are running for cover. They had friends or friends of friends who were killed or injured in the train bombing. They resent having been misled about who carried out the attack and you've broken the cardinal sin – you've been caught."

Holmes began to realise that the chance of avoiding a long term at His Majesty's Pleasure were slim. And he knew it wouldn't be pleasant. He was aware that Belmarsh had a reputation for housing some of the most violent prisoners; thankfully, mainly in a prison within the prison. But he was also aware that it held a high percentage of black and Asian offenders – men who would have good reason to resent him even if he hadn't blamed Arabs for the train bombing.

Along the corridors, James was returning to his cell after exercise. The group stopped to wait for a Prison Officer to unlock a gate. Two of the prisoners stood between James and the Officer – blocking him from intervening as the others attacked James with razor blades stuck into toothbrushes, slashing him around the face and throat. As he collapsed from the assault, his aggressors kicked him wherever they could.

Another officer pressed a panic button; alarm bells started to ring, metal implements were rattled against steel doors, gates and railings and men began to shout and jeer and boots crashed against the floor as reinforcements arrived to quell the disturbance.

The attack was over in less than four minutes but James lay unconscious on the floor, one member of staff administered first aid while they waited for help from Health Care who quickly sped him away to the small operating theatre on site.

When Homes heard about his deputy's injuries, he prayed he'd recover. Together, they might be able to watch each other's backs. If he was left on his own, he didn't think he'd survive to stand trial.

Chapter 64. Myth Busting

Michelle was in the kitchen preparing dinner while Zoë was on her laptop in the lounge.

"Shit," Zoë exclaimed "Fuck the media, fuck the haters, fuck the fucking police."

"What's up?" Michelle asked.

"Have you seen this report of a trans girl murdered near Warrington? The police have arrested a boy and a girl, both fifteen years old. But they're saying there's no evidence of it being a hate crime. Are they totally effing blind?"

"I saw that at the weekend, though there was no mention of the victim being trans in the first reports."

"Sixteen years old, hadn't even really started to live. So bloody sad. I once saw a report that said transgender people in the UK are 22 times more likely to be murdered than the average person. I had hoped those statistics had started to improve – but that doesn't seem to be the case. We're an easy target for anyone these days. You don't know how lucky you are to be cisgender."

Michelle was tempted to challenge Zoë's comment but the fact was that she was fortunate. Her history was well hidden, and needed to remain that way.

"Ah, seems there are some vigils being set up for the victim including one in Sackville Gardens on Wednesday. Must go to it," Zoë announced. "Might get a few allies along as well as trans people."

"Count me in, too," said Michelle as she carried the dinner plates to the table. "Pour the wine, will you?"

"Seems everywhere we look, these days, there are attacks on trans people. Whether it's because of one prisoner serving a sentence for sexual offences being moved to a female prison because they claim to be trans – when there's no evidence of them having transitioned previously so they don't qualify under prison service rules. Or suggestions that men will pretend to be women to gain access to female changing rooms or toilets if self-identification is allowed – in spite of the fact that there are already two dozen countries that allow self-identification without any such instances. It's like Brexit again with lies and myths being accepted. Or, worse, like the way Jews were treated in Germany in the 30s with no one challenging the misleading claims," Zoë said in a monotone; her eyes staring into the distance.

"Is it really as bad as that?" asked Michelle.

"Look at the facts. Theresa May planned to include transgender in a ban on Conversion Therapy; Johnson then announced it wouldn't be covered and went on to support a ban on trans women competing in elite swimming. When he resigned, Sunak's previous anti-trans statements were regurgitated. Other candidates also expressed anti-trans sentiments. The Equality and Human Rights Commission held private talks with anti-trans groups. There's been a 56% rise in transphobic hate crime. Waiting lists for the gender clinics are now years – is that coincidence?"

"A lot of the anti-trans campaigning is by right-wing religious, well, so-called religious, groups in the USA with huge resources behind them – their leaders flying around in private jets and living in mansions. I mean, what chance do we have against them?" Zoë added.

Over the next week, Michelle watched the number of planned vigils grow and the news coverage show hundreds of attendees at many of them – even in small communities. The police admitted that they were now investigating whether the attack was hate-related and there were increasing reports that the 16-year-old had been subjected to bullying at school because she was transgender. There was a clear ground swell of support for the victim and her family – and for the right of trans people to exist in peace. She saw an online appeal for the family attract thousands of donations and raise a six-figure sum. When she and Zoë reached the Gay Village on the Wednesday evening, they were unable to get close to Sackville Gardens due to the huge crowd that had turned out.

After the vigil, Michelle and Zoë met up with some of Zoë's trans friends for a drink.

"Ideally, what we need to do, is run our own campaign to challenge the myths that the gender critical mob are spouting. Maybe if we all sung from the same hymn sheet, instead of having different angles we want to get across, we'd be more effective," said Sophie, a statuesque fifties something transwoman with well-coiffured brown hair streaked with highlights.

"The problem is we have too many egos amongst those capable of speaking convincingly – often with their own personal agendas," Zoë pointed out. "It'd be like herding cats."

"So, what would you do if you could herd the cats?" Michelle asked.

"I guess the first thing is to agree on the key myths that are being spread around; then how to challenge each of those claims with clear evidence. For example, that there's a high percentage of detransition; that young people can start hormones before they reach puberty or have surgery, that we recruit people to be trans; that we are a threat to other women," added Adrianne, a petite blonde.

"Who do you see as targets to be convinced?" Michelle queried, taking a sip of her white wine after probing.

"Good question. The general public – especially women who might feel threatened; influencers, Members of Parliament and candidates from all parties; church leaders; journalists, just about everyone really," Zoë added.

"That's why you've got to prioritise. Go for those that might be in a position to resist moves to reduce trans rights or block changes that you want to fight for now or in the future," Michelle pointed out.

"Christ, it's an impossible task!" complained Sophie.

"Difficult, certainly, but not impossible. It's the proverbial elephant. You eat it one mouthful at a time – not try to deal with it in one go. Break down what needs to be done into manageable chunks first, prioritise the tasks and allocate resources. God, I sound like a Project Manager," Michelle remarked.

"Would you be prepared to give a hand with the planning, Michelle?" Zoë enquired, "You're the best Project Manager I've worked with. I know it's not your fight but will you help?"

"If I do, the first thing you need is agreement from as many community leaders as possible that they'll do whatever they can without letting personal ambition or egos getting in the way. You'll need to organise a conference to agree objectives and priorities. That'll need a venue," Michelle told them.

"This is going to cost a bomb. Isn't it?" asked Adrianne.

"If the community can raise more than a hundred thousand for a funeral – surely we can raise funds for our own survival," Sophie remarked. "Maybe we can get support in kind – office space, admin support and the like from other LGBT charities?"

"That's possible. There must be trans people with experience of fundraising. Hell, if transphobic groups can raise funds, surely we can do the same," added Zoë. "We could set up a crowdfunding page and approach other charitable foundations for support."

"I propose that we each think about what we consider our priorities should be, who we can approach and how — and meet up again at the weekend to allocate tasks and get moving. I suspect that we need to have a basic plan to put to community leaders for overall agreement and a discussion on strategy. If we go to them with a blank sheet of paper, my betting is that we won't agree on anything," said Sophie.

Michelle already had the kernel of a plan in her mind that she would develop in private.

Back home, Zoë poured Michelle a glass of wine and they sat down in the lounge.

"What do you think, Michelle? Are we wasting our time or is there a realistic chance of stopping the attacks on trans people?"

"There'll always be some who are transphobic and will do what they can to roll back trans and LGB rights. I think you need to focus on countering their false claims amongst the more reasonable and the uncommitted public who frankly don't give a damn about whether trans people have rights or not."

Michelle paused for a moment as she swirled the wine around the glass and took a sip.

"I'd say this breaks down into two main areas – political parties and groups specifically concerned with women's issues."

"What about Unions?" Zoë asked.

"Yes, them too," agreed Michelle.

"We could take stands at their national conventions. – and correct the misinformation the gender critical people are spreading. Need to ensure that anyone representing us is non-confrontational – otherwise we'll be accused of being men invading their space."

Michelle sat back and let Zoë present their ideas when the steering group got back together the following weekend. They'd also noted that the next general election was due by early 2025 and suggested having candidates stand against the main party leaders.

"It's a pity we can't put someone up in every constituency – we'd be able to target every household with leaflets but the deposits alone would come to more than three hundred thousand pounds and, realistically, we're likely to lose most if not all of them," Zoë remarked ruefully.

"We do think it's worth having stands at the party conferences – even the Tory one – to at least challenge the myths that are being used against us."

"So, how much are we looking at having to raise?" asked Adrianne.

"Between fifteen and twenty thousand," admitted Zoë. "We could do some work for less — say two party conferences and two women's conventions. That might be possible for five to six thousand. We'll just have to cut our coat according to our cloth. But come on. There are more than a hundred and fifty trans organisations in the UK. If each group raised forty quid, that's a start. Stonewall estimates there are six hundred thousand trans people in the UK. If each gave an average of a fiver, that would be three million pounds. With that, we could put someone up for every constituency, produce leaflets, a media campaign, employ staff, and take stands at dozens of events."

"Yes, well let's not get ahead of ourselves," said Sophie.

By the end of the day, the group had agreed what they saw as the priorities and a strategy to put to a wider meeting planned for the last weekend in March. They had also set up a crowdfunding page with an initial target of twenty-five thousand. The steering group were forced to meet again, however, to adjust their plans when a single deposit took the total raised to more than a hundred thousand.

"I had an email just before the deposit was made telling me to watch out for a large payment," Zoë messaged the others.

"Me too," replied Adrianne.

"And me," said Sophie. "It said we'd receive another email afterwards, has anyone had that yet?"

As she asked the question, her email application pinged.

"Something coming through now," she sent. The others confirmed that they'd also received a message from the mystery donor.

'I am a stealth transwoman who has been successful in business. I'm disgusted at how the media and politicians are treating the community and want to help – but I'm not prepared to out myself to do so. From the information you've circulated, you seem to have viable plans that I am prepared to fund up to one million pounds sterling, possibly more. The initial deposit was a gesture of good faith and intent. Any attempt to identify me will result in funding being withdrawn.'

Michelle read her copy sitting next to Zoë in their apartment. Not that she needed to, this seemed to her to be the most effective way she could use the Liechtenstein funds.

The End

Can I ask a favour?

If you enjoyed this novel, would you be kind enough to leave a review on any appropriate websites? They really do make a difference.

Thank you

Helen

About the Author

Helen identifies as female with a transsexual history - her preferred pronouns are she/ her. She grew up as a RAF Brat and dreamed of being a pilot herself but failed the medical due to having had hay fever (the RAF considered it risky trying to land an aircraft and sneezing at the wrong moment).

Throughout her childhood and early career in PR, advertising and marketing and getting married and having a family, she concealed the secret that she was transgender.

In 1998, Helen accepted that she needed to transition. Losing one job as a consequence, Helen joined Greater Manchester Probation as IT Help Desk Manager in 1999. As the first openly trans employee nationally she provided awareness training for probation and prison staff (and others) and became the de facto lead on trans issues.

Helen persuaded the then Lesbian and Gay staff association (LAGIP) to extend its membership criteria to include trans and bisexual members and spent several years as chair. She also helped to found a:gender - the UK pan-Civil Service trans support network and was made an honorary life member when she retired in 2015.

She served on local and national diversity boards and chaired a trans charity in Manchester as well as training as a counsellor. Her work was recognised with several awards including a Butler Trust Award presented by HRH Princess Anne at Buckingham Palace.

Since retiring, Helen has continued to present workshops on trans issues and provide counselling for trans individuals. She also became a volunteer with Diversity Role Models - going into schools and talking to students about homophobic, transphobic and biphobic bullying.

Overall, Helen estimates that she's met well over 1,000 trans individuals who would previously been described as transsexual and many more who do not plan to transition permanently including cross-dressers, gender fluid, non-binary, drag artists/drag queens and some who identify as she-male. The discussions she's had with all of these individuals mean she has a huge wealth of information to draw on for her stories to ensure that they are authentic.

Helen started writing short stories for Cross Talk, Northern Concord Trans Support Group magazine, in the mid/ late 1990s — and started to write a novel while she was 'between contracts'. That novel was put on hold when she started working for Greater Manchester Probation in 1999.

After surgery in 2000, she joined Spice, a social activity group, in Manchester and did a number of adventurous events with them. This led to her colleagues asking, on Monday mornings, what she'd done at the weekend.

Typical answers were driving a tank, flying a jet, sailing a yacht, riding a quad bike or a hovercraft. Her colleagues told her that she'd led such an interesting life, she should write her autobiography — so she did.

While recollecting memories for it, she recalled an incident when she was 19 and living in London. She'd taken the train to

Bournemouth, changing in the toilets at the end of the carriage and crossing over to Studland Bay and sunbathing in a bikini. She realised that she was being watched so left quickly.

But what if she hadn't noticed the guy?

What if he hadn't minded that she was trans?

That struck her as a possible start of a novel — which became 'Summer Dreams'.

Since retiring, Helen has been a member of the Manchester Women's Writers' Group which has provided valuable feedback on her work.

Check out Helen's website: www.helendaleauthor.info

Also by Helen

Fiction

Summer Dreams

"Summer Dreams" is an authentic story of the transgender community and illustrates the wide range of trans people's experiences, the problems, prejudices and fears that they face (and some of their own prejudices) — and the fact that being trans is just one facet of their lives. It was inspired by a true incident when the author was about 19.

But let Vicky tell you about Summer Dreams:

I was David, but now I'm Vicky.

I was sunbathing in sand dunes near Bournemouth in 2003, when Roger found me and changed my life. After spending a heavenly holiday with him as Vicky, I just couldn't face reverting to David. I knew, though, that becoming Vicky permanently was impossible.

There was only one option, I tried to kill myself.

Roger saved me then showed how life as Vicky was possible.

Summer Dreams tells of my transition journey, coming out to family and friends and their reactions, some of which were very difficult to deal with, especially Peter my twin brother's and the abuse we faced from him and others.

But being trans is just part of who I am. Roger and I have a normal life too.

But is it too good to last?

Summer Dreams is an adult novel with explicit sex scenes

It is set in 2003-8 when the terms transvestite and transsexual were commonly used.

ISBN

Paperback   978-1-9996329-3-9

What other readers have said:

"Brilliant"

"LGBT meets Howard's Way"*

"A page turner"

"Informs about trans issues without pushing it down the readers throat"

"It's a really good introduction to transgender issues and a romantic novel very well written"

"It's proper steamy"

"John didn't put it down beginning of lockdown, kept saying his glasses were steaming up"

"I really liked how Vicky was kind, caring and non-judgmental. Even though she's lucky, she still offers her help to Mia. Even though things seem to go smoothly, the book still shows the after thoughts and insecurities."

"An interesting viewpoint in the life of someone transgendered, the difficulties faced in life, and also in transition, many of which I had not considered. The basic storyline is sound, though I did find it a little 'wordy' in places, especially with the smaller details in regards to sailing, flying, and of routes to various places which seemed unnecessary to the story. Having lived in and around Southampton for 45 years I did enjoy, and imagined precisely, descriptions of pubs and places and I have been to. A good effort though for a first novel."

"Romance … and some sailing! This short novel follows Vicky as she falls in love with a man who seems too good to be true. But Vicky faces obstacles that you don't often read about in romance. She's a trans woman and we follow her through surgery, through the process of coming out to her family, via various yachting incidents, right through to… well you'll have to read it to find out. Great characters, a compelling story and a healthy dose of realism. Helen Dale tells it like it is and you can't help cheering for Vicky in all her trials, hoping that she gets to live 'happily ever after'."

Changes

A tale of corruption, blackmail, revenge, drug smuggling, murder, and self-discovery told from five points of view:

Nigel Hall has a comfortable life running his advertising agency and using girls and other activities including sailing and trips to casinos to entertain his clients.

George Collins enjoys perks that Nigel gives him and doesn't worry too much about the invoices he approves.

John Ives hadn't expected to take his cousin **Carol Ives**'s part as Cinderella in a panto when she injured her ankle horse-riding nor that photos from the event would later give his fiancée an idea for getting him in and out of her parents' house without their knowledge. Nor did he expect to discover how much he enjoyed cross-dressing or that his fiancée would support him.

Then **Mary Sanchez**, the widow of OJ, a former business partner of Nigel, returns from the USA. She takes over the company George works for and extracts revenge on Nigel, who she blames for OJ's death.

The consequences impact on all of them.

ISBN

Paperback   978-1-9996329-6-0

What other readers have said:

'A gripping page-turner

'Helen Dale has written a sexy, exciting novel as seen through the eyes of five well-rounded main characters. I especially liked John Ives who had to ask himself some very searching questions when he discovered he enjoyed dressing as a woman - although this did come in handy on more than one occasion.

''Changes' is a thrilling page-turner with a heart-pumping finale. I read a huge chunk of it during a long plane flight and I couldn't wait for the return journey so I could immerse myself in it again.

Impact

Part 1 of a proposed trilogy set largely in Manchester and the Gay Village in the late 1990s. The main character, Chris, is married with a daughter. The family have no idea that he cross-dresses. They live in Cambridgeshire but Chris is asked to manage a project in Manchester and rents a flat in Chorlton where he lives during the week. He returns home most, but not all weekends.

While in Manchester, he spends most of his time outside work as Christine.

His wife, Lucinda, is involved in an evangelical church with links to homophobic ministries in the USA.

Inevitably the two worlds collide.

ISBN

Paperback   978-1-7397667-1-9

What other readers have said:

"It was ironic that the Village had been created by a Chief Police Officer wanting to keep all the undesirables in one location. I drank a toast to him!"

So says Christopher Williamson about the Gay Village in Manchester when he is living a double life as Christine in 'Impact' (Book 1). I love the way the tension builds up as Christopher struggles with the thought of being 'outed' – thus losing his well-paid job and idyllic family life. The author paces the story well and it keeps you in suspense: Could Christopher ever stop dressing as a woman? Or was the urge he describes as being 'innate' and 'part of me' always going to prove too strong?

I thought the chapter headings were clever. They reference different aspects of 'food and drink'. And the fun-times Christine has with her new friends in the restaurants and clubs of Canal Street are often juxtaposed with Christopher's participation in barbecues and picnics with his family and long-standing neighbours at home.

These two lives are as different as you could possibly get, and Christopher's heartfelt dilemma makes for a fascinating read.

Operation Busted Flush
A Matter of Survival

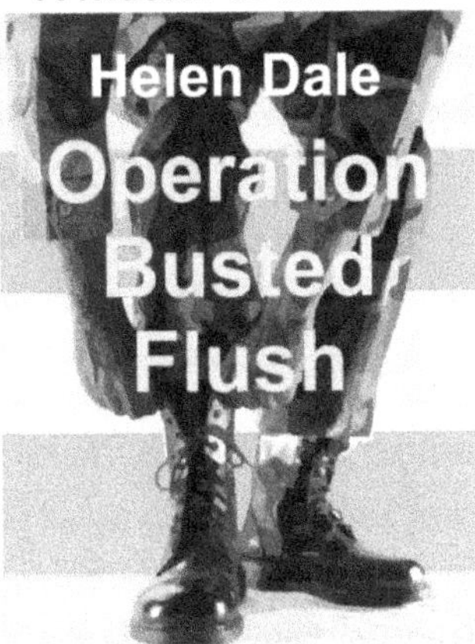

A group of trans veterans defend their
community from White House attacks.

'"And I say the time for waiting is over. He's tried to stop us serving in the military. He's tried to withdraw rights we've fought for. He wants to prevent us using appropriate washrooms. Now he wants to eliminate us completely – they've even taken down every reference to transgender off government websites for Christ's sake! Enough is enough. We have to f*****g do something!" Angela slapped her hand on the table.'

A group of ex-special forces transgender veterans decide to take action to defend their community against the White House's attack on transgender people.

ISBN

Paperback   978-1-9996329-5-3

What readers say:

"I thoroughly enjoyed this novella. It follows the antics of the President of the USA 2016 to 2020 and his aggressive attitude towards the LGBT community. A group of transgender ex-soldiers vow to take their revenge. I loved the scenes in the cabin where

they were plotting with military precision how enact their plan. I was with them all the way. There were also moments of tenderness – planning for a wedding and support for the grieving. I have very little experience of the trans community but now realise how hard they have fought for their rights in society and what a massive impact the attitudes of national leaders have on their everyday lives. A real page turner - I couldn't wait to hear what happened next and it kept you guessing to the very last page."

"Transgender avengers form a crack team to take down a corrupt and authoritarian US president before he causes more harm to their community. Good action-adventure romp with wish fulfilment for all those who have watched in despair over the past years as our hard-won trans rights are attacked by governments worldwide. Thoroughly enjoyed it."

Cross-over
Transgender Tales
Adventures and Misadventures on
a Journey from Transvestite to Transsexual

An online diary Helen kept between 1997 and 1999 when she first moved to Salford. She chatted to lots of other trans people online, many of whom had never been anywhere "dressed" so Helen invited them to visit and go down Manchester's Gay Village. This tells the story of those trips and others that she made with Vanity Club UK — a TV/TS club.

It also tells of her thoughts over that period when she started by identifying as transvestite but began to wonder if she was actually transsexual and if she would eventually need to transition permanently

There are descriptions of how Helen came out as trans to two of her oldest friends, at work and to her family — and the consequences of those steps.

It also includes:

- three stories that she wrote at the time for Northern Concord's magazine "Crosstalk" under the name Helen Williamson,

- A poem "Can You Tell Me What I Am?" which was written when I was questioning if I was TV or TS

- other humorous anecdotes from the period.

ISBN

Paperback   978-1-9996329-1-5

What readers say:

"Some great short stories about the dilemmas of being a TV in the early 80s 90s. The diaries reveal a hidden community proudly remembered for its peer support, mentoring and deep friendship. full of spirit and life."

Non-Fiction Books

A Tale of Two Lives

A funny thing happened on the way to the Palace

Inspirational story of award-winning trans activist, writer, trainer and counsellor: Helen Dale.

Having grown up as a RAF Brat and keen scout, dreaming of being a pilot in the RAF, she concealed a secret for decades before accepting, in 1998, that she needed to transition.

Losing one job as a consequence, Helen joined Greater Manchester Probation in 1999. As the first openly trans employee nationally she provided awareness training for probation and prison staff and others and became the de facto lead on trans issues.

She persuaded LAGIP, the then Lesbian and Gay staff association, to extend its membership criteria to include trans and spent several years as chair. She also helped to found a:gender - the UK pan-Civil Service trans support network and was made an honorary life member when she retired in 2015. Helen served on local and national diversity boards and chaired a trans charity in Manchester as well as training as a counsellor.

Her work was recognised with several awards including a Butler Trust Award presented by HRH Princess Anne at Buckingham Palace.

"A Tale of Two Lives" tells how she came out to family and friends and how that might have been handled better! It also covers her life after transition, embarking on a range of activities learning to scuba dive, qualifying as a yacht skipper, fire breathing, diving with sharks - including Great Whites - and holidaying around the world as part of a group or on solo trips showing that being trans is no barrier to living a full life.

Now available with colour Illustrations

A Tale of Two Lives is available as a paperback (with b/w illustrations) and as a hardcover with colour illustrations (depending on original photo).

ISBN

Paperback: (b/w illustrations):   978-1-9996329-7-7

Hardcover (colour illustrations):   978-1-9996329-9-1

What people have already said:

"an excellent read and filled in some of the gaps in your eventful life. It was a brave thing to write it but I would not expect anything less from you"

"I've read the book and found it very interesting, down to earth, no holds barred, and for me personally extremely helpful in understanding a close relative in a similar situation. Well done, I look forward to the next one."

"A book about journeys and self-discovery and how to weather life's ups and downs. Fascinating insights into Helen's transition story richly peppered with the fullness of family, friendship, work and really living life to the full. Yes, Helen you have made a difference"

"I really enjoyed this book which covers the very interesting life story of Helen.

"It's a really good read and keeps you interested as well as explaining more about the TV/TS community and the struggles they can face. Highly recommended"

"I loved this book and as my son is experiencing some of the same issues it gave me insight. I also bought the book for him which I think helped, though he has chosen not to transition. He chose instead to tell his closest friends and felt able to do that."

Helen Dale has been involved in the trans community for more than twenty years; initially providing support on the internet then training as a counsellor and counselling supervisor; chairing trans and LGB&T support groups and providing workshops on trans issues to a range of audiences — and has won several awards for this work.

This guide has been developed from those workshops and her personal experiences supporting other trans individuals.

It is intended to be easy to read keeping jargon to a minimum and explaining terms in simple language. The information is laid out in logical sections — with a comprehensive contents section to find relevant details easily.

With the number of individuals identifying as trans, intersex, non-binary or gender fluid doubling about every five years, if you haven't previously met or had dealings with a trans individual, you may well do before long whether as a manager or support worker friend or family. It will help you to identify the questions that you need to ask and how to avoid common mistakes. It will also be a valuable resource for anyone who identifies as transgender, intersex, non-binary or gender fluid.

The book is aimed at anyone dealing with trans people:

- Counsellors / Help-line Operators/ Befrienders
- Support/ Social Workers
- Union Staff
- Teachers and Lecturers
- Citizens Advice Bureaux
- Samaritans
- Criminal Justice System staff including
- Equality and Diversity Practitioners
- HR staff
- Other Managers
- LGBT+ organisations
- Family & Friends
- And Trans Individuals themselves

Contents include:

- Definitions
- Causality
- Social Transition
- Transsexual Journey to Surgery
- Travelling on: Post Transition / Surgery
- Trans Issues in Counselling
- Partners and Families
- Case Studies
- Legal History
- Discrimination & Hate Crime/ Incidents
- Employment
- Trans People in the Criminal Justice System
- Bibliography

Hard cover version includes colour illustrations; paperback version illustrations are black and white.

ISBN

Paperback (B/w illustrations):   978-1-9996329-3-9

Hardcover (colour illustrations):   978-1-9996329-8-4

What readers have said:

"Your books were the first thing I found that made sense from a human point of view instead of science and big words."